STALKING

BOOKS BY BLAKE PIERCE

A JESSIE HUNT PSYCHOLOGICAL SUSPENSE SERIES
THE PERFECT WIFE (Book #1)
THE PERFECT BLOCK (Book #2)
THE PERFECT HOUSE (Book #3)
THE PERFECT SMILE (Book #4)
THE PERFECT LIE (Book #5)
THE PERFECT LOOK (Book #6)

CHLOE FINE PSYCHOLOGICAL SUSPENSE SERIES
NEXT DOOR (Book #1)
A NEIGHBOR'S LIE (Book #2)
CUL DE SAC (Book #3)
SILENT NEIGHBOR (Book #4)
HOMECOMING (Book #5)
TINTED WINDOWS (Book #6)

KATE WISE MYSTERY SERIES
IF SHE KNEW (Book #1)
IF SHE SAW (Book #2)
IF SHE RAN (Book #3)
IF SHE HID (Book #4)
IF SHE FLED (Book #5)
IF SHE FEARED (Book #6)
IF SHE HEARD (Book #7)

THE MAKING OF RILEY PAIGE SERIES
WATCHING (Book #1)
WAITING (Book #2)

LURING (Book #3)
TAKING (Book #4)
STALKING (Book #5)

RILEY PAIGE MYSTERY SERIES
ONCE GONE (Book #1)
ONCE TAKEN (Book #2)
ONCE CRAVED (Book #3)
ONCE LURED (Book #4)
ONCE HUNTED (Book #5)
ONCE PINED (Book #6)
ONCE FORSAKEN (Book #7)
ONCE COLD (Book #8)
ONCE STALKED (Book #9)
ONCE LOST (Book #10)
ONCE BURIED (Book #11)
ONCE BOUND (Book #12)
ONCE TRAPPED (Book #13)
ONCE DORMANT (Book #14)
ONCE SHUNNED (Book #15)
ONCE MISSED (Book #16)
ONCE CHOSEN (Book #17)

MACKENZIE WHITE MYSTERY SERIES
BEFORE HE KILLS (Book #1)
BEFORE HE SEES (Book #2)
BEFORE HE COVETS (Book #3)
BEFORE HE TAKES (Book #4)
BEFORE HE NEEDS (Book #5)
BEFORE HE FEELS (Book #6)
BEFORE HE SINS (Book #7)
BEFORE HE HUNTS (Book #8)
BEFORE HE PREYS (Book #9)
BEFORE HE LONGS (Book #10)
BEFORE HE LAPSES (Book #11)

BEFORE HE ENVIES (Book #12)
BEFORE HE STALKS (Book #13)
BEFORE HE HARMS (Book #14)

AVERY BLACK MYSTERY SERIES
CAUSE TO KILL (Book #1)
CAUSE TO RUN (Book #2)
CAUSE TO HIDE (Book #3)
CAUSE TO FEAR (Book #4)
CAUSE TO SAVE (Book #5)
CAUSE TO DREAD (Book #6)

KERI LOCKE MYSTERY SERIES
A TRACE OF DEATH (Book #1)
A TRACE OF MUDER (Book #2)
A TRACE OF VICE (Book #3)
A TRACE OF CRIME (Book #4)
A TRACE OF HOPE (Book #5)

STALKING

(The Making of Riley Paige—Book 5)

BLAKE PIERCE

BLAKE PIERCE

Blake Pierce is author of the bestselling RILEY PAGE mystery series, which includes sixteen books (and counting). Blake Pierce is also the author of the MACKENZIE WHITE mystery series, comprising thirteen books (and counting); of the AVERY BLACK mystery series, comprising six books; of the KERI LOCKE mystery series, comprising five books; of the MAKING OF RILEY PAIGE mystery series, comprising five books (and counting); of the KATE WISE mystery series, comprising six books (and counting); of the CHLOE FINE psychological suspense mystery, comprising five books (and counting); and of the JESSE HUNT psychological suspense thriller series, comprising five books (and counting).

ONCE GONE (a Riley Paige Mystery—Book #1), BEFORE HE KILLS (A Mackenzie White Mystery—Book I), CAUSE TO KILL (An Avery Black Mystery—Book I), A TRACE OF DEATH (A Keri Locke Mystery—Book I), and WATCHING (The Making of Riley Paige—Book I) are each available as a free download on Amazon!

An avid reader and lifelong fan of the mystery and thriller genres, Blake loves to hear from you, so please feel free to visit www.blakepierceauthor.com to learn more and stay in touch.

TABLE OF CONTENTS

PROLOGUE

Kimberly Dent turned her collar up against the cold. She was out later than usual, but it was just a short, safe walk home from her friend Goldie Dowling's house. The night wasn't uncomfortably cold, and Kimberly liked the way the air stung her cheeks and she could see her frosty breath. It was actually very pretty, with the streetlights shining on what was left of last week's snowfall.

Kimberly was sure her parents wouldn't mind that she was out so late. Her high school grades were good, and Mom and Dad trusted her to stay out of trouble—not that there was a lot of trouble to get into in a boring little town like Dalhart. Besides that, both of her parents would surely be asleep by now. Like most people in this neighborhood, they were always early to bed.

She was humming a pop tune, but she realized she didn't know what the song was.

Something new I heard on the radio, I guess.

It felt odd that a song she didn't even really know could get stuck in her head like this, but it seemed to happen a lot lately. Of course, someday that song would be as familiar as an old pair of shoes. And yet she'd never be able to remember exactly where or when she'd heard it for the first time.

The thought made her sad somehow.

But then, the whole evening had seemed kind of sad.

She and Goldie had done all the usual things they'd shared over the years— painted each other's nails, arranged each other's hair, danced to some of their favorite songs, played cards, watched some TV.

But then they'd gotten cross with each other—or at least Goldie had gotten cross with Kimberly.

And over nothing, Kimberly thought.

All Kimberly had done was ask Goldie whether she was sure she wanted to stay here in Dalhart after they both graduated this spring. Goldie had snapped at her about that.

"Are you saying I shouldn't go right ahead and marry Clint?" Goldie had demanded.

Kimberly had been startled. She knew that Goldie and Clint were serious about each other. They'd been together since back in middle school. But Goldie hadn't said anything about marriage before. And if Clint had proposed to Goldie, she sure hadn't mentioned it to Kimberly.

Of course, Kimberly knew it would make Goldie's parents happy if she married Clint and settled down right here in Dalhart and started having kids pretty much right away. But that had never seemed like Goldie's style.

At least not until tonight.

Then Kimberly had made the mistake of reminding Goldie of her longtime dream of heading out to New York or L.A. and becoming an actress.

"Oh, grow up," Goldie had said. *"We're too old for those kid dreams anymore."*

Those words had hit Kimberly hard—but not as hard as what Goldie said next.

"Or do you still think you're going to be an Olympic gymnast?"

Kimberly had been shocked. No, she hadn't dreamed about that since she'd been twelve or thirteen. It had seemed cruel of Goldie to bring it up out of nowhere.

Still, Kimberly did hope for a lot more than Dalhart had to offer. She was anxious to get out of here. She figured she'd move down to Memphis right after graduation and take any kind of job she could get and enjoy city life for a change.

She hadn't mentioned that to anybody yet—not even to Goldie, and tonight certainly hadn't seemed like the right time to tell her. Kimberly was sure her parents were going to be against any idea like that. She just hoped she'd be strong enough to stand up for what she wanted when the time came for her to leave.

She was halfway home now, and she was still humming the same tune and wondering what it was. Then she heard a strange, high-pitched sound. At first she thought it was the wind. But there was hardly even a breeze in the air.

She stopped in her tracks and listened.

Someone's whistling! she realized.

Not only that, but someone was whistling the same tune she'd been humming.

Suddenly the whistling stopped.

She called out softly but firmly, "Is that you, Jay? If it is, this isn't very funny."

Her boyfriend Jay had broken up with her about a week ago, and he'd been behaving like a creep ever since. Word had gotten back to her that he'd even been badmouthing her to his male friends, complaining that she wouldn't "put out" for him. Of course that had been why Jay had ended their relationship, but Kimberly sure didn't think it was anybody else's business.

And now she couldn't help but wonder—was Jay stalking her?

She sighed and thought, *I wouldn't put it past him.*

She shook her head and started to walk again.

Then the whistling resumed.

Walking faster now, Kimberly looked all around, trying to figure out where the sound was coming from. She simply couldn't tell. But she was starting to hope that it was Jay after all. She didn't like the thought that it might be one of Jay's freaky pals. And she didn't dare imagine that it might be somebody she didn't even know.

As she kept walking, she looked around at all the houses where people she'd known all her life lived. Should she knock on one of those doors so somebody could let her inside?

No, it's late, she thought.

She didn't see any lights on inside the houses. Those people were probably all asleep by now. Even if they weren't, they wouldn't be pleased to be disturbed at this hour. And her parents would have a fit if they heard she'd been bothering people so late at night.

The whistling stopped again, but Kimberly took no comfort in that. The night now seemed colder and darker and scarier than it had just a few minutes before.

As she turned a corner, she saw a van parked a short distance ahead. Its lights were on and its engine was running.

She breathed a sigh of relief. She didn't recognize the vehicle, but at least it was *somebody*. Whoever was driving the van would surely give her a ride the short remaining distance to her house.

She walked up to the vehicle and noticed that its side door was open. She peered in and saw that the bare, open interior was separated from the front seats by some kind of metal fencing. She didn't see anybody anywhere inside.

Kimberly wondered whether the driver might be having engine trouble and maybe had gone looking for help. If it was a stranger from out of town, they'd have no idea who to turn to.

Maybe I can help, she thought.

She reached for her cellphone in her purse, figuring she could call her dad. But then she hesitated for a moment, uncertain whether she really wanted to wake Dad up, even to help out a stranger.

She heard approaching steps and turned to see a face that she recognized.

"Oh, it's you . . ." she said, feeling a moment of relief.

But the expression on his face froze any words that might have followed. She had never seen his eyes so cold and hard like this.

Without saying anything at all, he reached out a hand and snatched her purse and phone away.

Now fear rose up in Kimberly's throat. All the things she thought of doing flashed through her mind.

Scream for help, she told herself. *Wake someone up,*

But suddenly she was lifted and shoved violently backward into the van.

The door slammed and the interior lights went out.

She groped for the door handle, but found that it was locked.

Finally Kimberly found her voice again.

"Let me out of here!" she screamed, pounding on the door.

Then the driver's door opened, and the man climbed inside.

The van began to move.

Kimberly grabbed hold of the wire fencing that separated her from the driver and demanded, "What are you doing? Let me out of here!"

But the vehicle was on its way down the street now, and Kimberly knew that no one in the sleepy neighborhood could hear her.

CHAPTER ONE

When the first shot rang out, Riley Sweeney reacted fast. Just as she'd been trained back at the Academy, she dropped down behind the nearest barrier—a Honda that was parked in front of the motel where two killers were holed up. But she didn't feel that the compact vehicle offered her a lot of protection.

It was cold this time of year in upstate New York, and snow was falling. Visibility wasn't at all good. This was Riley's first armed standoff, and she didn't feel sure that she'd even survive it.

Peering through the swirling flakes, Riley saw that Special Agent Jake Crivaro was more safely ensconced beside a hefty SUV. Crivaro, her partner and mentor, looked worried as he glanced back at her. Riley wished she could silently signal him that she'd be all right. Like the six local cops who had arrived with them just now, Riley and Crivaro were wearing Kevlar. But Riley knew better than to expect too much from her protective vest. A well-aimed shot to her head—or even an accidental shot—could be fatal.

Crivaro lifted a bullhorn to his lips and called out, "This is Special Agent Jake Crivaro with the FBI. I'm here with my partner and local law enforcement. We've got you surrounded. There's no way out. Come out with your hands up."

No reply came from the motel room where the two killers were holed up. Instead, there was just an eerie whistle of wind.

Riley cautiously poked her head out from behind the little car, trying to glimpse the motel room. Just then came sharp crack coupled with a shrill, piercing sound—something between a whistle and a buzz.

A bullet had whipped right past her. Riley pulled her head back out of sight. She gasped as she realized, *I just got shot at for the first time.*

She'd had plenty of training with live ammunition, but none of it had been aimed at her personally.

Just as Crivaro and the cops had done, she'd already drawn her weapon—a .40 caliber semiautomatic Glock.

The weapon felt clumsy in her hands.

She reminded herself that she ought to be glad she'd recently graduated to something more powerful than the .22 caliber pistol she was given when she received her FBI badge. But this one was less familiar, and she didn't yet know what she was going to have to do with it.

She did know better than to return fire now—and apparently so did everyone else on the team. They'd do everything they could to end this situation without unnecessary gunfire.

She suspected that some of the cops who were gathered nearby felt the same way. Maybe some of them were as new to this as she was. Ever since she'd completed training for the FBI last year, Riley had wondered how she'd feel when she got into this kind of situation for the first time.

And now that she was in the middle of it, she still didn't know.

One thing she felt sure of—she didn't feel panic. In fact, she didn't feel afraid at all. It was more as if she were outside her body watching what was going on, like some sort of dispassionate observer. The situation seemed completely unreal, almost dreamlike. But she knew that her whole body was flooded with adrenaline, and she had to keep her wits about her.

She felt a little bit encouraged that at least one person on this team had some idea of what he was doing. This was far from Agent Crivaro's first experience of this kind. The short, barrel-chested man was a legend in the Agency for his long record of closing tough cases.

Riley leaned against the car, waiting for some sign of what she should do. In the moments of silence, she thought back to gathering at the local police station with this team. It had been just a little while ago, but right now it seemed like days or even weeks had gone by since then. They'd all been fully briefed about the killers they were going to try to apprehend.

When she'd seen pictures of the pair, she'd thought, *Kids. Just a couple of kids.*

Seventeen-year-old Orin Rhodes and his fifteen-year-old girlfriend, Heidi Wright, had started their killing spree just days ago in the nearby town of Hinton. It had begun with a simple act of pure desperation.

Heidi had called Orin by phone to tell him she was in danger at home. Orin had gotten his father's gun and gone to Heidi's house, where he'd found her being sexually assaulted by both her father and her brother. Orin had killed both of the girl's attackers.

Then Heidi had grabbed her own father's gun, and she and Orin had gone on the lam. Finding themselves short of cash, they'd tried to rob a liquor store. But the robbery had gone bad, and they'd wound up killing both the store manager and an employee.

The police weren't sure exactly what had happened next. They knew the kids had turned up in the town of Jennings, where they'd tormented and killed two perfectly innocent people—a middle-aged handyman and a seventeen-year-old girl. Then the killer pair had disappeared again.

That was when the local authorities had called for FBI assistance. They'd found the teenagers' behavior so puzzling that they'd specifically requested someone from the Behavioral Analysis Unit.

Riley and Agent Crivaro had flown in from Quantico to do whatever they could to help. It was clear to them that Orin and Heidi had gotten some kind of pleasurable rush from the impromptu murders. They likely craved more of the same. They no longer needed reasons for killing, and their spree wasn't going to end soon.

By the time Riley and Crivaro had analyzed the situation, the local cops had determined that Heidi and Orin were hiding out in this motel. The two agents had joined the local team that went to capture them... or to kill them if necessary.

Now here they all were in this parking lot with snow falling around them. One of the teenagers had greeted their arrival with a shot from the motel room window, and now a second shot had been fired, narrowly missing Riley herself.

What now? Riley wondered.

Agent Crivaro spoke through his bullhorn again in what sounded almost like a sympathetic, kindly tone.

"Orin, Heidi, don't make this worse than it already is. We don't want trouble. All we want to do is talk. We can work this out. Just come outside with your hands where we can see them, both of you."

Another silence fell before a young man's voice called out from the window. "We've got a hostage."

Riley felt a chill of alarm. Agent Crivaro's expression showed that he felt the same way.

3

Orin continued, "It's a motel maid. She says her name is Anita. Don't try anything or we'll kill her."

Agent Crivaro peered cautiously from behind the SUV and called back, "Let us see her."

No reply came. Riley could guess what Crivaro was thinking.

Is Orin bluffing?

Maybe they didn't have a hostage at all. Maybe they were only stalling, trying to put off their inevitable capture. They certainly weren't behaving as if they really had a hostage. Riley had studied and trained in hostage situations at the Academy, so she had a pretty good idea of what to expect.

The kids ought to be negotiating right now, insisting on some sort of safe passage away from this location. But that wasn't what was happening. The whole situation seemed to have come to a standstill.

Then Riley could hear voices inside the hotel room. It was impossible to make out what was being said, but it sounded like the boy and girl were arguing. Then Heidi's voice called out through the window.

"Okay, we'll let you see her. Just don't try anything."

Riley looked out from behind the car again. She could see the motel room door open. Then a figure stepped into the doorway. It appeared to be a woman wearing a hooded winter jacket. Her face was impossible to see in the swirling snow. She stood still in the doorway, holding her hands shakily above her head.

Orin Rhodes called out from inside the room, "Okay, there she is, you've seen her."

Crivaro spoke back on his bullhorn, "Yeah, but you really don't want to do things this way. Believe me, I know what I'm talking about. I've seen it happen lots of times. Keeping a hostage only makes things worse for you. Just let her go. Let her come over here with us. Then we can negotiate some sensible solution."

Riley doubted Crivaro's ploy was going to work, and she suspected that he felt the same way. Why would the couple give up the only leverage they had at a moment like this?

Then, to Riley's surprise, the woman took a couple of steps toward them. Her heart jumped up in her throat as she heard Orin growl some kind of inaudible protest. Riley couldn't see him, but he clearly didn't like what was happening.

Is he going to shoot her? she wondered.

But the woman took a few more faltering steps away from the motel. Maybe, Riley thought, Orin and Heidi had finally lost their taste for killing. But Riley felt even more uncertain than ever about what was happening. If the couple actually let the hostage go, what would they do next? What *could* they do?

They could surrender, Riley thought.

Or they could fight.

Of course, it would be suicide if they did. Riley had some idea of what to expect if shooting started. The couple really didn't stand a chance in an actual gunfight, not against a team like this. They weren't likely to withstand a hail of bullets, and they'd surely run out of ammunition long before the team did. The ultimate choice was to surrender or die.

The woman walked silently across the sidewalk, then stepped off the curb onto the parking lot pavement. Riley watched Crivaro, wondering what her mentor might do next. Would he step out to greet the woman, then make sure she was hustled away to a place of safety? At the moment, he showed no sign of budging from his crouching position behind the SUV.

Then the woman's steps quickened alarmingly. She drew close to Riley, apparently without seeing her there.

And now Riley could see the woman's face. It wasn't a hostage at all. It was Heidi Wright herself and she was whipping something out from her jacket.

She's got a gun, Riley realized.

Riley knew what she had to do, but even so she hesitated.

The girl's gun blazed, scattering ill-aimed shots across the barriers that hid the cops and agents. Then she spotted Riley. She smiled a weirdly innocent smile as she turned her weapon toward the young agent.

For what seemed like an interminable split second, Riley stared at the barrel of the pistol. Then she realized that she had already raised her own weapon and aimed it squarely at the center of Heidi's chest.

Riley fired a single shot.

Heidi staggered backward, and the pistol fell from her hands. Her smile disappeared, replaced by what appeared to be an expression of shock and dismay. Then she tumbled into a heap onto the ground.

Riley could hear Orin's voice cry out, "Heidi!"

She turned and saw several cops rushing toward the motel doorway. With a look of stunned horror, Orin emerged from the room. He raised his hands high as he stared across the parking lot at his stricken girlfriend. He remained completely docile as one of the cops put him into cuffs and read him his rights.

Seized with a deep horror, Riley walked toward the girl's body. Blood gushed out of the wound in her chest, staining the layer of snow on the pavement. Heidi's eyes were wide open, and her mouth worked silently as she gasped her final breaths. Then she fell completely still. The look on her dead face seemed inexpressibly sad.

Riley began to shake all over, and her own gun almost fell from her hand. Suddenly, Agent Crivaro was at her side, and he gently took the weapon away from her.

Riley felt completely numb now.

She heard herself say, "What have I done?"

Crivaro put his arms around her shoulders and said, "You did good, Riley. You did what you had to do."

But Riley could only repeat, "What have I done?"

"Come on, let's get you where you can sit down," Crivaro said.

Riley could barely stay on her feet as Crivaro gently led her away toward a police van. She could still feel the dead girl's eyes staring at her.

I killed someone, she thought.

She'd never killed anyone before in her life.

And now she had no idea how she was going to deal with it.

CHAPTER TWO

When Riley's fiancé, Ryan Paige, tried to put his arm around her shoulders, she pulled away. It wasn't the first time tonight that she'd reflexively drawn back from his touch. She was sure it hurt his feelings, but she couldn't help it.

After the shootout in Jennings, Riley had returned to Quantico with Jake and then made the drive back to DC. She was sitting beside Ryan on the couch in their little basement apartment, but the images in her mind were from the earlier part of that long day.

Riley could still see Heidi Wright's dead eyes staring into the snowfall, and she couldn't shake off her feelings of guilt. She knew she was being irrational, but she didn't feel deserving of anyone's affection right now.

"What can I do?" Ryan asked.

"Nothing," she replied. "Just sit here with me."

They sat together in silence, and Riley felt grateful for Ryan's presence. They'd had their differences during the last few months, but right now he seemed very much like the handsome, earnest, and considerate young man she had fallen in love with during her last semester in college.

Meanwhile, her mind went back over all that had happened since she'd shot Heidi. It had all been a blur, and during the flight back to Quantico Agent Crivaro had kept telling her she was in a state of shock.

I still am, I guess, she thought.

She still had all the physical symptoms of shock, including cold, clammy, sweaty hands and recurring dizziness and confusion.

How long would it take before those symptoms went away?

In a dull monotone that had sounded strange even to her, she'd just now told Ryan about the whole incident. It was all she could do not to relate the events in the third person. It was hard to use the words "I" and "me" to describe her own actions. She kept wanting to believe the whole thing had happened to someone else.

When she finished Ryan said in a gentle voice, "There's one thing I still don't understand. I guess it kind of makes sense that Heidi pretended to be a hostage, at least for a few moments. It was a desperate bluff. But why did she come right on out into the parking lot? Why did she try to...?"

Ryan's voice faded, but she knew the words he couldn't bring himself to say.

"Why did she try to kill you?"

Riley remembered the moment when the girl had stood in the motel room doorway before taking those fatal steps into the parking lot, and how she'd heard Orin's inaudible protests.

She said to Ryan, "Orin didn't want her to go outside like that. He tried to talk her out of it. But I guess she thought... she realized... it was over. She wanted to go out..."

Her own voice faded as a stupid cliché froze on her lips.

"... in a blaze of glory."

Ryan shook his head.

"I can't imagine how you feel about it," he said. "But good God, Riley, she and her boyfriend killed six people. You can't say she didn't deserve what happened to her."

Riley felt as though she'd been slapped across the face at the sound of that word.

Deserve.

Right now she herself felt so painfully undeserving of Ryan's consideration or even affection. It hadn't occurred to her to think of Heidi Wright as deserving what Riley had done to her.

Is Ryan right? she thought.

She thought over what little she knew of the girl's life—a life of unthinkable cruelty and abuse, apparently. Heidi and her boyfriend had started on their murder spree when her own father and brother sexually assaulted her. Riley couldn't blame Orin for killing those men. Then, after that, both Orin and Heidi must have felt too desperate to have any idea what they were doing.

And too young as well, Riley thought.

Once again, Riley couldn't help remembering Heidi's fresh, smiling face at the moment when she'd pointed her gun at Riley—the moment before her own death.

Riley murmured aloud, "Heidi was just a kid, Ryan. She didn't deserve to die like that. What she deserved was a better life than the one she got stuck with."

Ryan looked at Riley with an uncomprehending look.

"But you didn't have any choice," he said. "If you hadn't fired when you did, you'd surely be . . ."

His voice trailed off again. Riley knew the word he just couldn't say.

Dead.

"I know," Riley said with a sigh. "That's what Agent Crivaro keeps telling me. He says it was justified. It was even proper procedure. It was self-defense, a clear case of 'imminent danger of death or serious bodily harm.'"

"Crivaro's right, Riley," Ryan said. "Surely you know that."

"I know," Riley said.

And rationally, she *did* know. But at some primal level, she couldn't accept that judgment. She felt as though her whole body was accusing her right now. She wondered if she could ever get over this feeling.

Ryan gently touched her hand, and Riley let him hold it. Ryan's hand felt almost hot against the chilly sweat in her palm.

Ryan said, "Riley, how often are you going to have to go through this?"

"It's my job," Riley said.

"Yeah, but . . . what kind of job is it that makes you feel so terrible about yourself? Is this really what you want to do with your life?"

"Somebody has to do it," Riley said.

"Does that somebody have to be you?" Ryan asked.

Riley had no idea how to answer that question. And as much as she appreciated Ryan's concern, she couldn't be sure how sincere he really was. Who was Ryan really troubled about deep down—Riley or himself?

She hated to doubt him like this, but she couldn't help it. During the short time they'd been together as a couple, she'd learned to her dismay that Ryan had a selfish streak. And he had plenty of selfish reasons to hate what she was doing these days. He even hated the commute Riley took to Quantico every day. It deprived him of the use of his prized Ford Mustang and forced him to use public transportation to get to his job at his law office every day. He'd hadn't hidden from her the fact that he found that humiliating.

Ryan squeezed her hand and said, "Maybe you should just think about a change. We can live off my paychecks. We've even started a savings account. Even if you stayed at home—and I know you don't want to do that—I could still support us both. I could even move us into nicer place someday soon. You don't have to do this . . . for us."

Riley said nothing.

Ryan said, "Maybe this is something you should talk through with your counselor."

Riley winced sharply. She regretted having mentioned to Ryan that she had to go to at least one therapy session. After she and Crivaro had gotten back to Quantico, Special Agent in Charge Erik Lehl had told her that counseling was mandatory now that she had used deadly force for the first time.

She hadn't made an appointment yet.

Ryan said, "Riley, I'm worried. What are you going to do? What are *we* going to do?"

Riley was startled to feel a twinge of impatience.

She said, "Ryan, do we really have to talk through this right now?"

Looking chastened, Ryan patted her hand and said, "No, of course not. I'll go fix us some dinner."

"No, I'll do it," Riley said.

"Don't be ridiculous," Ryan said. "You need to take it easy. I'll take care of everything. Do you want me to bring you a drink?"

Riley nodded, and Ryan went on into the kitchen. A few moments later he came back out with a glass of bourbon and ice and set it on the coffee table in front of Riley. Then he went back into the kitchen and rattled around as he started to fix supper.

Riley really wished he'd let her do the cooking tonight. She needed something, anything, to do with herself. She positively dreaded having all of tomorrow off.

As she sat alone on the couch sipping her bourbon, she felt a rising surge of emotion. Before she knew it, she was sobbing. She tried to keep it quiet so Ryan wouldn't hear her and come back and try to comfort her.

She didn't want to be comforted.

All she wanted to do was cry.

During the flight back to Quantico, Agent Crivaro had told her again and again that it was all right to cry.

"Go ahead, let it out," he'd kept saying.

But somehow, she just hadn't been able to do that—not until right now. And now it felt good to just let her feelings pour out after such a long, horrible day. She cried and cried until she felt limp from it.

When the tears finally stopped flowing, Riley figured she'd better go to the bathroom and wash her face so Ryan couldn't see her like this. But before she could get up from the couch, the apartment's landline phone rang.

She heard Ryan call out, "I'll get it."

"No, I will," she called back.

She was closer to the phone than Ryan. And even a trivial task like answering the phone felt good right now—although she couldn't imagine that the call was from anyone she could possibly want to talk to.

When she picked up the phone, she heard a familiar voice.

"Hey, kid. How're you doing?"

Riley's spirits suddenly rose as she recognized that voice. It was her roommate from her days at the Academy, Francine Dow.

"Frankie!" she stammered with surprise. "It's—it's good to hear from you!"

Riley hadn't seen Frankie since they'd graduated in December, and they'd only talked by phone a couple of times. After graduation, Frankie had been assigned to work as an agent at the FBI's DC headquarters.

With a voice filled with concern, Frankie said, "Go ahead, talk to me."

Riley was startled.

She stammered, "Do you mean . . . you know . . . ?"

"Yeah, I know what happened. And you'll never believe how I found out. I got a call from Special Agent Jake Crivaro himself. He said he was worried about you. He said you might need to talk to a friend."

Riley smiled to hear a note of awe in Frankie's voice. Although Riley hadn't realized it when Agent Crivaro first took an interest in her unique abilities, she'd since learned then that her mentor was something of a living legend in the FBI. Frankie couldn't seem to get over her amazement that Riley was now his fulltime partner.

Getting a phone call from him must have blown Frankie's mind, Riley thought.

Frankie said, "So how are you feeling?"

"Not good," Riley said with a sigh. "I guess I always knew . . . I'd have do something like this someday. But I didn't know how bad it was going to feel."

"Well, I wondered if maybe you'd like to get together and let off some steam," Frankie said.

Riley felt a surge of gratitude.

"Oh, that would be wonderful, Frankie," she said. "I've got tomorrow off. How does lunch sound?"

"Sounds great," Frankie said.

After they made plans and ended the call, Riley stood staring at the phone in her hand. Something was just now sinking in.

Agent Crivaro reached out to Frankie.

He called her about me.

It was a surprising and incredibly thoughtful thing to do, and Riley felt deeply touched by her mentor's concern. And tomorrow's lunch date with Frankie gave her something to look forward to after such an awful day.

Feeling suddenly much better, Riley walked into the kitchen.

She thought, *I'm going to help Ryan with dinner, whether he wants me to or not.*

Today had been worse than she had ever imagined. But she had friends who were helping her through it. Maybe tomorrow would be easier. After all, what kind of nightmare could be worse than the one she'd just faced?

CHAPTER THREE

Before noon the next day, Riley went outside to wait for Frankie to pick her up for lunch. She found herself wondering if she would actually be able to talk with her Academy friend about what had happened yesterday. Ryan had gone to work as usual, happily taking the opportunity to drive their car to his office for a change. So Riley had slept late and had a leisurely morning.

Soon Frankie pulled up in her beat-up hatchback, and Riley climbed in. She realized that her friend's ruddy features and rusty-colored hair were a welcome sight. She told herself that this was definitely going to be a better day.

Frankie drove them to their favorite DC lunch spot, Tiffin's Grub & Pub. They sat down at a little table and both ordered tuna melt sandwiches. Then they sipped coffee and exchanged some small talk, avoiding the topic of Riley's first kill.

Maybe we won't get around to talking about it, Riley thought.

If so, she felt fine with that. Spending some time with Frankie was going to be enough to make her feel a whole lot better. Meanwhile, she and her friend had some catching up to do.

Frankie said, "So I hear you've worked three more cases since we last saw each other. That's pretty impressive. Word's getting around that you're quite a prodigy—the next Jake Crivaro, they say."

Riley blushed at what she knew to be high praise.

"I've still got a lot to learn," she said. "So how's your life here in DC? How is being an FBI agent working out for you?"

Frankie frowned and sighed.

"It's not all I hoped it to be, I guess," she said.

Riley felt a pang of concern. She knew that Frankie had spent six months working as an undercover drug agent before she'd even entered the academy. Because of her past experience, Frankie had been assigned to an FBI drug enforcement team after graduating. Riley knew that Frankie had been excited and hopeful about the assignment. Now she sounded sad and disappointed.

As their sandwiches arrived, Riley asked Frankie to tell her about it. Frankie took a sip of coffee and thought for a moment.

Then she said, "You know, I learned just one real lesson back when I working as an undercover cop in Cincinnati. I learned that the whole 'War on Drugs' is completely wrongheaded. It's a war that can't be won. The real problem is, there's a lot of pain out there, and a lot of unhappy people. Locking them up for using drugs doesn't get to the root of the problem. And I guess I . . ."

Frankie's voice faded away for a moment.

Then she said, "Well, I thought I could make a difference, working in the FBI. I thought I could change how things got done. But it's not working out that way. It's all the same-old same-old, just like in Cincinnati. The only difference is, now I'm not working undercover anymore. But I'm still involved in the same kinds of operations, and I can't change anything. I'm feeling like a naïve chump for thinking I could make a difference."

Riley leaned across the table toward her friend and said, "Frankie, give yourself some time. You're just getting started. Be patient."

Frankie scoffed. "Yeah, well, patience isn't exactly my strong suit. And anyway, my problems seem pretty trivial next to what you went through yesterday. Crivaro sounded really worried about you over the phone. Do you want to talk about it? Do you want to tell me what happened?"

Riley hesitated for a moment. Then she figured talking about it was part of why she was here. As she began to tell Frankie everything that had happened yesterday, she felt a lump in her throat.

Don't start crying again, she thought.

She managed to keep her tears in check as she described the moment when she killed Heidi Wright.

Then she said, "Frankie, she was just a kid—fifteen years old. It wasn't her fault that she'd had such a rotten life. She didn't have any good choices. She was desperate. She needed someone to give her a good home and some guidance and some love. She didn't deserve to die like that."

Frankie's face was full of concern now.

"I don't suppose there's any point in my pointing out the obvious," Frankie said.

Riley nodded and said, "I know, I know. I didn't have any choice. It was her life or mine."

"And your life matters, Riley," Frankie said. "It matters a lot."

Riley had to wipe away a tear now.

"I feel like things will never be the same again," she said.

Frankie tilted her head and said, "Well, I've never had to shoot anybody, but...I know what it's like to do something that really changes you. I've been there. I understand."

Riley knew what terrible event Frankie was referring to. Back when she'd been working undercover in Cincinnati, a drug dealer had forced Frankie to shoot up with heroin at knifepoint. She'd had no choice.

Riley remembered what Frankie had told her about the incredible euphoria she'd experienced.

"If I'd died right then, I'd have died happy."

That was the event that had convinced Frankie that the "War on Drugs" was pointless. Riley knew that Frankie would be struggling with that experience for the rest of her life. Until now, Riley hadn't been able to imagine what it was like for her.

Maybe now I can understand, she thought.

Riley took a bite of her sandwich and thought for a moment.

Then she said, "Here's the strange thing, Frankie. About two weeks ago, I really *wanted* to kill someone. It took all my self-control not to do it."

"What happened?" Frankie asked.

Riley said, "Maybe you heard about that case Crivaro and I worked on in Maryland."

"Yeah, that was a nasty business," Frankie said. "The killer's name was Mullins, right?"

Riley nodded. "Yeah, Larry Mullins. He killed two little kids he was hired to take care of—suffocated them in two different playgrounds."

Then with a slight groan she added, "Of course, Mullins hasn't been convicted yet. His trial date hasn't even been set and the evidence we've got against him is still thin. But Crivaro and I know he did it—and so do the kids' parents."

Riley paused for a moment, dreading the memory she was about to describe.

"Mullins is a smug bastard," she said. "He's got this oozing baby-faced innocence about him, which is why the kids' parents trusted him. I hated his guts the moment Crivaro and I caught him. He grinned at me, practically admitting with his eyes that he was guilty. But he also knew damn well it was going to be tough for us to prove it."

Riley drummed her fingers restlessly on the table.

She said, "And right then and there, when I was putting him in cuffs and reading his rights, he smirked and said to me, 'Good luck.'"

Frankie gasped a little.

Riley continued, "God, you have no idea how angry that made me. I really wanted to kill him. I think I actually reached for my Glock. Crivaro touched me on the shoulder and gave me a warning look. If it weren't for Crivaro, I might have blown Mullins away right then and there."

"It's a good thing you didn't," Frankie said.

"Maybe so," Riley said. "But now I can't help wondering—what if Mullins had been my first use of deadly force? Surely I wouldn't feel as bad as I do now. Maybe I'd even be okay with it. Instead, I wound up shooting some poor dumb kid who didn't stand a chance in life. It's just..."

Riley gulped down an ache of anger and bitterness.

"It's just not fair," she said.

Riley and Frankie sat eating silently for a few moments.

Finally Frankie said in a cautious voice, "You know, you'll probably think I'm crazy for saying this but... maybe we're both better off the way things happened to us."

Riley's eyes widened.

"What do you mean?" she asked.

Frankie shrugged and said, "Well, if I hadn't been forced to shoot smack that one time, I'd never have realized how stupid the War on Drugs really is. And if you'd been able to kill Larry Mullins, maybe you'd find it easy to use deadly force in the future—way too easy."

Frankie fell silent, then wiped a tear from her eye.

"I know we're both hurting, Riley," she said. "But I think maybe it's better to hurt than get hardened against pain. At least we've been able to keep our humanity, our vulnerability, everything that's best about us. A lot of people in our line of work don't manage that."

Riley nodded slowly. She knew that Frankie was saying exactly what she needed to hear right now. She realized she was definitely lucky to have Frankie to commiserate with today. This was better than any therapy she was likely to get.

She and Frankie ate quietly for a little while.

Then Frankie asked, "So how are things going with that fiancé of yours? Have you set a wedding date yet?"

Riley was startled by the question.

She stammered, "Uh, no, not yet."

"No?" Frankie said, giving Riley a skeptical look.

"Not yet," Riley repeated, then kept on eating in silence.

She felt uneasy at what Frankie must be thinking right now. She remembered something Frankie had said to her when they'd first met...

"I've got kind of a jaundiced view of men in general."

Although Frankie rarely talked about it, Riley knew that Frankie's own four-year marriage had ended in a bitter divorce. Frankie probably didn't have any reason to expect things to work out with Riley and Ryan.

Is she right, maybe? Riley wondered.

After all, things hadn't been especially good between them lately.

Riley and Frankie chatted about little things as they finished their meal. When Frankie was driving her back to her apartment, Riley found herself dreading the rest of her day off, especially wondering how things were going to be with Ryan this evening.

She wondered—what did it say about her that she didn't look forward to seeing her own fiancé? Perhaps worse, was she getting hooked on the dangers and ordeals of her work?

She only knew that she couldn't help how she felt.

If I don't get back to work, I'll lose my mind, she thought.

Whatever was waiting for her out there, she needed to go ahead and face it.

CHAPTER FOUR

Jake tapped his foot uneasily as he sat across the desk from the Special Agent in Charge at the Behavioral Analysis Unit.

It sure sounds like a serial, he thought.

Erik Lehl was describing a pair of similar murders in Kentucky and Tennessee. Jake was trying to decide if he wanted to even think about this right now. After all, he'd been involved in a shootout in upstate New York just yesterday.

Lehl wound up his account and said, "Agent Crivaro, the only reason I'm talking to you about this is that I don't have any other senior BAU agents to send out there right now."

Jake chuckled and said, "So I'm a last resort, huh?"

Lehl didn't laugh at Jake's little joke. Of course, Jake was well aware that his boss wasn't known for his sense of humor.

"You know you're not," Lehl said. "I just don't want to send any rookies. But I know you might need a break after what happened yesterday. If so, I'm fine with that. It's not exactly a high-profile case, at least not yet. I can get the FBI field office in Memphis to handle it. But the local sheriff is in kind of a panic and he specifically requested BAU. I'd feel better about things if I knew I had my best agent on the job."

"You shouldn't flatter me, sir," Jake said with a smile. "It'll go to my head."

Again, Lehl didn't laugh. The lanky man steepled his lengthy fingers together and gazed at Jake expectantly.

"I'll do it," Jake finally said.

Lehl appeared to be genuinely relieved.

"All right, then," Lehl said. "I'll get a plane ready to fly you to the Dyersburg Regional Airport. I'll arrange for some local cops to meet you there. Do you want me to assign you a partner?"

Jake fidgeted in his chair.

"Naw, I'll handle this one on my own," he said.

Lehl let out a slight growl of dismay.

He said, "Agent Crivaro, I believe we've talked about this."

Jake was amused by Lehl's parental tone, as if his boss was gently scolding him.

"Yeah, I know," Jake said. "You keep telling me it's time I learned to play nice with others. But I'm old and fixed in my ways, sir. If you send me out with a rookie, I'll only terrorize the poor bum. I might send him screaming into the night. You wouldn't want that."

Then came a rather ominous pause.

I guess he doesn't approve of my answer, Jake thought.

Finally Lehl said, "Just consider taking a partner. I'll get back to you about that flight."

The meeting ended, and Jake walked back to his own office. He sat down at his desk, which was cluttered with the work he'd been doing today. He'd been poring over the "nanny killer" case in Maryland, trying to put together enough evidence to convict a child murderer named Larry Mullins. He and Riley had arrested the man a couple of weeks ago.

The trial was going to be scheduled soon. Although Jake, Riley, and their whole investigative team knew for a virtual fact that Mullins was guilty, he was worried about whether a jury would agree.

Jake wondered whether he should have said no to Lehl just now. Lehl wouldn't have held it against him. And it wasn't as if he didn't have anything else important to do. Besides, he was still rattled after the events of yesterday.

I guess I'm just a guy who can't say no, Jake thought.

He wondered whether he might be addicted to working in the field, and to all the action and danger that sort of work involved.

Or maybe it was something else.

Lately he'd felt his confidence in his own field abilities slipping. His uncertainty about the Mullins case made him feel those doubts more acutely. Maybe he'd accepted this case out of some anxiety to prove he could still do his job— not just well, but better than anyone else in the BAU.

But what if those days are over? he wondered.

He thought back to something Agent Lehl had just said.

"Just consider taking a partner."

Jake suspected that it was good advice. Trying to go solo while struggling with self-confidence issues might not be a good idea. But Lehl had just told him that he didn't have any senior agents available. Jake didn't feel like giving on-the-job training to some dumb, green rookie—not when a serial killer was probably at large and getting ready to strike again.

Of course, there was one new agent Jake didn't feel that way about…

Riley Sweeney.

His young protégé was more than merely promising. She already had better skills than many much more seasoned agents, even if her judgment was sometimes still erratic and she had trouble following orders. Someday, he knew, she'd be as good if not better than he himself had ever been. He liked knowing that she could carry on his work after he was gone. And he liked working with her.

But more than that, he felt as if he might be starting to really depend on her. If it was true that his own abilities were declining, having Riley on hand made him feel more secure about his work.

But as Jake considered the matter, he sighed aloud.

I can't ask her to work on this case, he thought.

It was way too soon. The poor kid was much too traumatized after the events of yesterday. Ever since the shootout in that snowy parking lot, Jake had been haunted by the stricken look on Riley's face as she'd stared down at Heidi Wright's body.

The dead girl looked even younger than her actual fifteen years—like a pathetic, broken little doll. Although Riley hadn't said so, Jake knew that she couldn't help thinking of herself as some sort of murderer. The poor kid had still been in shock the last time he'd seen her yesterday.

Of course, Jake and Riley had both known that she was going to have to use deadly force sooner or later. But Jake had never imagined that it was going to happen under such awful circumstances—and of course, Riley hadn't either.

She needs some time off, Jake thought.

She also needed the kind of professional counseling that Jake was in no way prepared to give her.

And yet Jake wondered whether he really had the right to make such a decision on her behalf. Shouldn't she be allowed to decide for herself whether she felt ready to get back to work?

Another question troubled him deeply.

Can I really do this job without her?

Jake reached for his desk phone and punched in her number.

Riley was walking into her apartment when her cellphone rang. Frankie had just driven her home from Tiffin's Grub & Pub, where the two friends had enjoyed a delicious lunch and some quality conversation. Riley hoped the call wasn't going to sour her mood.

As Riley shut the door behind her, she looked at the phone. The call was from Jake Crivaro. She answered it immediately.

She heard her mentor's gruff voice say, "Riley—Crivaro here."

Riley smiled at his familiar salutation.

She almost said, *I know.*

Instead she said, "What's going on?"

She heard Crivaro grunt indecisively. Then he said, "Uh, I just wanted to know . . . when I last saw you yesterday, you weren't feeling well. Are you feeling better?"

Riley felt a spark of curiosity. She felt sure that Crivaro was calling about something more than her well-being.

"Yeah, I'm feeling better," she said. "I guess I've got a long way to go, though. Yesterday was . . . well, kind of tough, you know?"

"I know," Crivaro said. "I'm sorry things turned out that way. Have you made a counseling appointment yet?"

"Not yet," Riley said.

"Don't put it off."

"I won't," Riley said, not at all sure she really meant it.

An awkward pause ensued.

Then Crivaro said, "Well, I thought I'd let you know that I'm flying out to Tennessee in a little while. There have been a couple of murders, one in Kentucky and one in Tennessee, and they sound like they might be the work of a serial killer. Lehl put me on the job."

Riley's curiosity grew. This seemed like an odd bit of information for Crivaro to want to share with her right now.

"I hope it goes well," she said.

"Yeah, well..."

An even longer silence fell.

Then Crivaro said, "Lehl says I should work with a partner on this case. He's got nothing but rookies available, so I thought I'd call and ask...Naw, it's a bad idea, forget I said anything."

Riley felt a tingle of excitement.

"Do you want me to come with you?" she asked.

"No, I shouldn't have called, I'm sorry. I'm sure it's the last thing you want to do right now. You need to rest, spend some time with your fiancé, get your head back to normal. You also need to get some counseling under your belt before you come back to work. You know that sooner or later, you'll need to go through that psych evaluation."

But not right now, Riley thought. *Not if I'm already away somewhere on another case.*

She blurted, "I'll do it."

She heard Crivaro sigh.

"Riley, I'm really not sure about this."

Riley said, "Well, I'm sure. Who else can you work with? You need someone tough, someone who knows you. You'd only terrorize some poor rookie."

Crivaro chuckled nervously and said, "Yeah, that's kind of what I told Lehl. Anyway, he's getting a plane ready to fly to Tennessee. Do you want me to drive to DC and pick you up?"

"No, you don't need to do that," Riley said. "I can get there faster by train. I know the schedule, and there's one I can catch soon. If you pick me up at the Quantico station, we could go directly to the airstrip."

Riley gave him the arrival schedule and Crivaro replied, "Okay, then."

After a hesitation he stammered, "And, uh..."

Riley sensed that he was struggling to find the right words for what he wanted to say.

Finally he simply said, "Thanks."

Riley almost found herself saying, *"No, thank you."*

Instead she said, "I'll be there soon."

She ended the call and sat down on the couch, staring at her cellphone. She felt startled by the decision she'd just made. She really hadn't given the matter any thought at all.

Did I just make a mistake? she wondered.

She didn't feel like she'd made a mistake. In fact, she felt deeply relieved. She was surprised by her own eagerness to get back to work.

But what surprised Riley most about the call was Crivaro's tone, almost like a shy schoolboy asking a girl on a date.

He really wants to work with me, she thought.

He doesn't want to work with anybody else.

It gave her a warm feeling to be wanted—and perhaps even needed.

But when she got up from the couch to head for the bedroom to fetch her always-ready go-bag, something occurred to her.

Ryan.

She had to call him to let him know. And she doubted that he was going to take it well. She remembered their conversation last night, and how he'd pressed her about quitting the BAU, and what she'd said in reply.

"Ryan, do we really have to talk through this right now?"

They hadn't gotten around to it yet, of course. There simply hadn't been any time. But now Riley was heading out to work on a new case anyway.

She picked up the landline phone and nervously punched in Ryan's phone number. He sounded cheerful when he answered the phone.

"Hey, sweetie, I'm glad you called. I've got reservations for tonight at that restaurant we both love, Hugo's Embers. Isn't that great? You know how hard it is to get a table there."

Riley gulped anxiously.

She said, "Yeah, that's great, Ryan, but…we're going to have to do this some other night."

"Huh?"

Riley fought down a sigh.

"Agent Crivaro just called," she said. "He wants me to work with him on a case in Tennessee. I'm leaving right now to catch a train to Quantico."

A tense silence fell.

"Riley, I can't say I like this," Ryan said. "Are you ready to go back to work? You were in pretty bad shape last night. And besides…"

There was another pause.

Then Ryan said, "Riley, we need this. A romantic evening together, I mean. It's been a long time since we…you know."

It took Riley a moment to understand exactly what he meant.

Then she realized, *Oh my God. He's talking about sex.*

How long had it been since they'd made love? She didn't know, and realized she hadn't thought about it at all lately. Between the two cases she'd already worked on this month, she'd been exhausted. Besides that, she'd been preoccupied with the upcoming Mullins trial.

She said, "I'll make it up to you, I promise."

"Riley, that's not the point. You decided this without even talking to me."

Riley felt a twinge of anger.

Am I going to have to consult Ryan every time I take a case?

But the last thing she wanted was to get into a fight with him about it right now. She simply didn't have time.

She said, "I'm sorry about this. I really am. We'll talk things through when I get home."

"I don't want you to go," Ryan said in an imploring voice.

"I've got to go," Riley said. "It's my job."

"But—"

"Goodbye, Ryan. I've got a train to catch. I love you."

She ended the call and slumped with sigh of despair.

Should I call Crivaro back? she wondered.

Should I tell him I can't do the case?

Crivaro would surely understand. He'd told her as much already.

But then Riley felt a surge of resentment. Ryan had no business pressuring her like this, especially after what had happened yesterday. She had work to do, and she couldn't spend the rest of her life asking Ryan's permission to do it.

She hurried to her bedroom, got her go-bag, and headed out to catch the train.

CHAPTER FIVE

To Riley, life was beginning to feel like one long plane trip with Jake Crivaro. They had just flown back from New York yesterday evening. Now they were on the BAU jet again, headed for the western end of Tennessee.

It's almost like I never came home at all, she thought.

In a way, she wished that were true. It would be nice to realize that her argument with Ryan over the phone this morning had just been a dream, and that things were just fine between them.

Unfortunately, she knew that all of it had really happened.

And of course, so had the terrible events of yesterday.

My whole life seems like a bad dream right now, she thought. *Like a nightmare of endless flying, danger, and sudden death.*

She shook off her dark thoughts and looked at Crivaro. He was sitting next to her going over some handwritten notes that he'd taken about their upcoming case.

He explained, "About a week ago, a body was found in the woods near Brattledale, in Raffel County, Kentucky. The victim was a teenage girl, Natalie Booker."

"How was she killed?" Riley asked.

"Strangled," Crivaro said. "If it was just a one-off in just one state, it wouldn't be any of our business. But yesterday another body turned up, another teenager, named Kimberly Dent, also strangled, and probably by the same killer. Her body was in the edge of some woods near Dalhart, Tennessee—across state lines."

"Which makes it an FBI case," Riley said. "If we wanted to take it up."

"That's right," Crivaro said. "Aside from that, the Raffel County Sheriff Ed Quayle asked specifically for help from BAU, so we're definitely involved."

Crivaro folded up his notebook.

"That's about all I know so far," he said. "Sheriff Quayle will be meeting us at the airport, and I'm sure he'll have more to say."

Riley nodded in agreement, and she and her partner fell silent for a while. As she sat staring out the window, her mind began to drift back to yesterday's awful shootout.

Riley heard Crivaro say in a gentle voice, "You look tired."

She turned toward him and saw that he was looking at her with concern.

"I guess I kind of am," Riley said. "I didn't get much sleep last night."

"Are you sure you're up to working on this case?"

"I'm sure," Riley said.

But she really didn't feel so sure about it. And she could tell by Crivaro's worried expression that he sensed her doubts.

He said in a gentle voice, "It was a tough thing, what happened to you yesterday."

Riley shrugged and said, "I guess you know how it feels."

"Not really, no."

Riley was surprised to hear him say that.

Hasn't he ever killed anybody? she wondered.

Crivaro hadn't needed to use deadly force on any of the cases Riley had worked with him on so far. The closest he had come was when a madman was about to inject Riley with a deadly dose of amphetamine. But Crivaro's then-partner Mark McCune had fired the shot that felled the killer.

Nevertheless Riley was sure that Crivaro must have used deadly force during his twenty-plus years as an FBI agent—probably many times.

But there had to be a first time, she thought.

Maybe it would help her to hear him tell her about it.

She asked in a cautious tone, "Agent Crivaro . . . could you tell me about the first time you had to use deadly force?"

Crivaro shrugged. He didn't look especially unsettled by the question.

"Well, that's some ancient history," he said. "Have you ever heard of the Magrette bank robbery of 1980?"

Riley's eyes widened.

"Of course I've heard about it," she said. "I learned about it at the Academy. I've even acted out parts of it with other cadets. It's still used in anti-terrorism and survival training. Were you involved with that?"

Crivaro smiled an odd sort of smile.

"Yeah, toward the end of it, anyway. Do you want to hear about it?"

Riley nodded silently.

Crivaro said, "Well, tell me everything you know about it already. I don't want to bore you with stuff you've heard a zillion times."

Riley almost scoffed aloud. There was nothing boring about the story of the Magrette robbery.

Nevertheless, she said, "Well, I know that the whole thing was crazy—and extremely violent. A gang of six bank robbers stormed into a bank in Magrette, Pennsylvania, armed to the teeth and wearing military fatigues. They forced the tellers to hand over $20,000 in cash."

"A lot of money back then," Jake said.

"But the local police got word about it while it was going on," Riley said. "When they showed up at the scene, a gunfight broke out right there in front of the bank."

Jake shook his head.

"Those poor cops," he said. "They had no idea how outgunned they were."

Riley said, "A deputy got hit—five times, if I remember right."

"He survived, amazingly enough," Crivaro said.

"The robbers managed to get to their getaway vehicle," Riley continued. "Then they led the cops on a wild chase. The robbers fired at the police cars, even threw homemade bombs at them. All kinds of vehicles got damaged, including a police helicopter. The robbers managed to get away for a time."

Crivaro grunted slightly.

"Yeah, and that was when the FBI got called in—me included," he said. "Early the next morning, a team of us tracked the gang down to some nearby woods, but it turned out to be an ambush. We were met by a hail of bullets. Our team chief, Val Davidson, was killed instantly."

Crivaro shuddered and added, "Got hit with a bullet from assault rifle. Pretty near took his whole head off. I'd never seen anything like it."

He fell quiet for a moment, and his gaze seemed to turn inward.

Then he said, "We all returned fire, including me, although we only got glimpses of our attackers in those woods. The gunfire seemed to be coming from everywhere and nowhere. I fired the very last shot, though. The split second I fired, I heard a cry of pain from the woods. Then all the shooting stopped, and everything got quiet."

Crivaro shuffled his feet nervously.

He said, "Then five of the robbers came toward us with their hands above their heads. They were surrendering! Another guy and I went out into the woods to try to figure out what happened. We found Wallace Combs, the gang leader, lying dead on the ground, killed by a bullet square in the center of his chest. The rest of the gang soon told us that Combs had talked them into fighting to the death. But as things turned out, they couldn't go on without him."

Crivaro squinted, as if struggling anew with his disbelief.

"I'd killed him," he said. "But I'd never even seen him. I'd just been shooting out into the woods. It was the luckiest damn shot in the world."

Crivaro fell quiet for a moment.

"I can't say I ever felt guilty about it," he said, "but it changed me. It made me harder, I guess. Part of it was seeing my chief get killed like that. I've never had trouble using deadly force ever since then."

Then he looked Riley squarely in the eye.

He said, "It's a different experience for everybody—that first kill, I mean. What happened to me that day—well, it was completely different from what happened to you yesterday. I didn't see the man I shot until he was dead. It didn't feel so personal, so . . . well, I don't really have any idea how you feel about it."

Riley winced sharply at those words.

For a moment, she again saw that innocent young face staring with dead eyes into the snowfall. As helpful as it had been to talk about this with Frankie a while ago, Riley knew that she still had a lot to deal with.

And it's going to take time, she thought.

Crivaro patted her on the shoulder.

"So do you want to talk about it?" he said.

Riley thought for a moment, then shook her head no.

"That's probably just as well," Crivaro said. "I'm not the guy who can help you get through this. I don't have the right touch. You really need to talk to a therapist, just like Lehl ordered you to do. Promise me you'll make that appointment as soon as we get back to Quantico."

"I promise," Riley said.

But she felt a sharp dread as she said those words.

She wondered how she could open up about such an awful experience to a total stranger. How could it possibly help?

And why is it anybody else's business, anyway?

Can't I get out of it somehow?

But of course she knew she couldn't. Orders were orders, and a promise was a promise.

And anyway, she and Crivaro were about to pursue a probable serial killer.

I probably have worse things to dread than a visit to the doctor, she realized with a bitter smile.

CHAPTER SIX

The tall, grim man waiting for Riley and Crivaro when they got off their plane didn't seem at all welcoming. Riley guessed that this must be Sheriff Quayle, who had actually requested their help. But he was just standing there on the tarmac of Hayden Regional Airport with arms crossed and an angry expression on his face. He looked as if he thought Riley and Crivaro had already done something he didn't like.

Does he think we're late or something? Riley wondered.

It seemed to her that they'd gotten here as quickly as they reasonably could.

Riley and Crivaro produced their badges and introduced themselves. Quayle didn't bother to do so himself.

"Come on," he said in a gruff voice. "I'll drive you there."

Riley could only guess that "there" meant the crime scene.

A man of few words, Riley thought.

She and Crivaro followed him through the small airport terminal, then outside into the parking lot. The weather was about like it had been in Virginia—cold, but not bitterly so. Not the way it had been in upstate New York. But there was some snow on the ground and it was cold enough that Riley was glad she'd dressed warmly for the trip.

Riley, Crivaro, and Quayle climbed into a police cruiser marked "Raffel County Sheriff."

As he drove out of the parking lot, Quayle grumbled quietly, "It's a fine day when we need folks like you in these parts."

Riley gave Crivaro a curious glance.

"Why doesn't he like us?" she mouthed silently.

After all, as Crivaro had told her on the plane, Quayle had personally called the FBI and requested an investigation, even specifying that he needed BAU agents. Crivaro smiled slightly at Riley and shrugged, as if to wordlessly suggest that he'd explain this to her later.

Then Crivaro said to Quayle, "What can you tell us about the murders?"

"Not much—not yet," Quayle said. "That's why you're here."

"Did the victims know each other?" Crivaro asked.

"Not that their parents knew of," Quayle said. "It's possible, I guess. It's only a ten-minute drive between Dalhart and Brattledale, and some people visit back and forth. Even so, folks in Dalhart tend to stay put, they keep among themselves. Kind of insular, you might say."

"What can you tell me about the local victim?" Crivaro asked.

Quayle let out a bitter sigh.

"Kimberly Dent was a good girl," he said. "A really great kid. I've known her since the day she was born. I went to school with both her dad and mom, Phil and Claudia—childhood sweethearts, they were. They're good folks. Nobody has ever said anything against them. But then, there's nothing but good folks around these parts. We don't get the kinds of problems you people are used to."

Riley didn't know exactly who or what Sheriff Quayle meant by "you people," but she did notice a note of contempt in his voice when he said those two words.

Quayle soon turned off the main highway onto a smaller rural route road. As they drove out into the countryside, Riley looked out the window at the pleasant, snow-covered rolling hills with bare trees scattered in clusters here and there. Although the landscape wasn't mountainous like it was where Riley had grown up in western Virginia, Riley felt reminded of scenes of her Appalachian childhood.

The drive stirred up memories in Riley—some of them nostalgic, but many of them sad. Much of her childhood had been difficult. especially after she'd seen her mother shot to death in a candy store. Riley had been just a little girl. Although she was deeply affected by the beauty of this kind of country, she'd learned at a very early age that beauty and ugliness often existed side by side.

And something very ugly happened here, she thought.

"It's coming right up," Sheriff Quayle said.

As they rounded one final bend, Riley saw a parked car and two people—a man and a woman—standing where the shoulder of the road was wide enough for vehicles to pull off. It looked like repeated traffic had dissolved most of the snow in that area.

The two people were both looking down at something standing just a few feet off of the road. It was a white cross, about a yard tall.

Kimberly Dent's parents, Riley suspected.

Her heart lurched a little at the thought of meeting the bereaved parents. She hadn't expected to have to do this already, and she was sure Crivaro hadn't either.

Sheriff Quayle pulled over onto the shoulder and stopped his car behind one already there. Riley and Crivaro got out with him and they walked toward the couple, who barely seemed aware of their arrival.

Riley could see the roadside memorial more clearly now. The simple painted wooden cross had Kimberly Dent's name written across it. Someone—the couple, Riley guessed—had placed a bouquet of artificial flowers in front of it. The couple stood there with their heads bowed as if they were in church.

The man was holding a mallet, so he must have just pounded the cross into the ground. The couple had surrounded the base of the cross with rocks in the shape of a heart.

The couple turned at the sound of Sheriff Quayle's voice.

"Phil, Claudia, I've brought some people I want you to meet."

Sheriff Quayle introduced Riley and Crivaro to Phil and Claudia Dent. Both Riley and Crivaro said they were sorry for their loss and apologized for having to ask them some questions right now.

Riley saw that Phil and Claudia both had thin, serious faces. Doubtless they looked more sad than usual, but Riley got the feeling that they didn't smile a lot even in better circumstances. She wondered whether their daughter had shared their serious demeanor. Somehow she doubted it. Without knowing quite why, Riley pictured Kimberly Dent as a typically cheerful and outgoing teenager.

In flat, expressionless voice, Claudia said to Riley and Crivaro, "I hope you can find out whoever did this."

"We'll do our best," Crivaro said. "Do you have any idea who might have wanted to harm your daughter?"

Phil said rather sharply, "Somebody who doesn't like *us.*"

Riley was startled by how he emphasized the word *us.*

Claudia said, "Not somebody from around here. Somebody from elsewhere."

She straightened herself up a little and added, "It's getting to be that kind of a world."

As Crivaro continued to ask the couple questions, Riley felt as though a few things were becoming clearer to her—including the sheriff's curt attitude toward them. She remembered something he'd said to her and Crivaro during the drive.

"We don't get the kinds of problems you people are used to."

He'd also said, *"It's a fine day when we need folks like you in these parts."*

From her own childhood, Riley knew that rural people could be "kind of insular," as Sheriff Quayle had put it, and set in some old-fashioned ways. But the outside world was changing fast, and changing all the time.

Riley suspected that Phil and Claudia felt as though the world was closing in around them these days, threatening their way of life. And now, their daughter's murder made them feel that way much more acutely.

They really don't want to think the killer is one of them, Riley thought.

Instead they wanted to think the killer was some outsider, someone who hated them for being the kind of people they were—someone from the world that Riley and Crivaro had just arrived from.

It saddened Riley to think that they might very well be wrong.

While Riley was thinking all this over, Crivaro had kept on asking the couple questions.

"Did Kimberly have a boyfriend?" Crivaro asked.

The parents winced slightly.

"No," Phil said.

"Absolutely not," Claudia added.

Riley exchanged curious glances with Crivaro. The couple sounded almost as if they found the question to be offensive.

Then Crivaro said, "What about a best friend? Another girl, I mean."

Claudia said, "That would be Goldie Dowling."

"Could you tell us how to get in touch with her?" Crivaro asked.

Sheriff Quayle said to Crivaro, "I can take care of that for you."

Crivaro nodded and told the couple that he didn't have any further questions for right now. He asked them to please get in touch with the sheriff's office if they thought of anything that might be important.

Claudia stepped back from the memorial, nodding with satisfaction at how it looked.

She said, "Folks will start bringing flowers and such to decorate it. It'll look very pretty. But I hope folks have got the sense not to bring real flowers. They'd die fast in this weather."

Then she frowned and added, "Anything alive would die if you put it here."

Riley heard a world of cold bitterness in those enigmatic words. As the Dents turned away and headed back to their car, Riley took note of two things. Phil and Claudia hadn't offered each other any physical affection or consolation. They hadn't so much as even held each other's hands.

Also, neither of them had cried.

Riley wondered whether that was unusual, especially for the woman. Then she remembered her own reactions after killing Heidi Wright—the numbness that had clung to her for hours and hours until she'd finally cried alone in her apartment.

Maybe she's done a lot of crying already, Riley thought. *Or maybe her grief hasn't really hit her yet.*

As the couple drove away, Sheriff Quayle said to Riley and Crivaro, "Come on, I'll show you where the body was found."

They began to walk toward the trees and underbrush on the far side of the shoulder.

Crivaro asked, "Do you have any idea what kind of vehicle the killer used?"

"No, and I don't know how we could tell," Quayle said, pointing to the ground. "The shoulder here is a thick layer of gravel, and there's hardly any snow on it. A vehicle wouldn't leave any tire tracks here to speak of."

Crivaro let out a scoff. He stopped walking and stooped down.

Riley realized what he was looking at. A telltale mound of fallen leaves was bunched up about where the gravel ended at the edge of the shoulder.

Crivaro swept away the leaves and said to Quayle, "Have a look."

Sure enough, Riley saw a partially obscured tire track in the dirt in the dirt where the gravel stopped.

"Someone parked here," Crivaro said, tracing the track with his finger. "He was smart enough to smudge up the tread marks so we couldn't get any solid forensic info from them. But the ground would have been cold and he was in a hurry. He even kicked some leaves over here to hide whatever might be left. His vehicle was heavy enough to leave traces. Not enough here to tell what kind of vehicle it was though."

Crivaro got back to his feet, and the three of them waded a very short distance into the barren brush at the edge of the shoulder.

Quayle pointed to the ground and said, "As you can see, there isn't a lot of cover this time of year, and she was wearing a red parka, so she was pretty much in clear view of the road. A driver noticed her early this morning and called us about it."

"When was the body taken away?" Crivaro asked.

"About noon," Quayle said. "The medical examiner didn't want to leave it exposed to the elements longer than necessary.

Riley could see where leaves were pressed down from where the body had been. Crivaro stooped down for a closer look.

Crivaro touched the ground and said, "Kimberly wasn't killed right here."

Quayle looked surprised.

"That's what the medical examiner said, based on the approximate time of death," Quayle said. "But how did you know that?"

Riley could see exactly what Crivaro meant. She knew what he was going to say as he gestured and pointed and explained it to Quayle.

"There's no sign of a struggle. The only disturbance is where the brush was tamped down where the killer carried the body here, and this indentation where the body was laid out. It looks like she was laid out pretty carefully, not casually dumped here. What else has your ME been able to determine?"

"Death by strangling, sometime yesterday," Quayle said. "He couldn't determine the exact time of death."

Crivaro said, "I hope you've got good photos of both crime scenes."

Quayle nodded and said, "Yeah, and the scenes look a lot alike. The sheriff over in Brattledale agrees, it's got to be the same killer. I'll show you the pictures when we go to the station."

As Crivaro and Quayle kept talking, Riley tried to focus her mind on her surroundings. Her unique talent was for getting into a killer's mind, usually at crime scenes like this one.

It was a weird ability, and seemed uncanny even to her. But Crivaro had often assured her that there was nothing psychic or mystical about it. Riley simply had exceptionally good intuitions and instincts—the same as Crivaro himself did.

Of course, it was easier to do when a crime scene was fresher and the body hadn't been taken away. But even here she got a slight tingle, an indistinct feeling of the killer's presence.

But she got no feeling of hostility or rage.

Was that because the killing had taken place elsewhere, perhaps many hours before the body had been brought here?

Had the killer gotten the hatred for the victim out of his system?

No, that's not it, Riley thought.

She sensed that the killer felt never felt any rage at all. After all, the body had been laid out in what appeared to be an orderly and perhaps even respectful manner.

What about guilt? Riley wondered.

No, she didn't pick up any feelings of guilt either. And as usual, her gut feelings were corroborated by the scene itself. The killer had left the body more or less out in the open, where it was sure to be found in the early morning hours. He hadn't had tried to hide his deed. He'd felt no shame at all.

Did he feel pride, maybe?

Riley couldn't tell. But she did sense that maybe he'd felt a certain satisfaction in what he'd done. When he'd left this place, he'd felt as though he'd done the right thing, perhaps even done his duty.

Riley shivered as another feeling came over her.

He's not finished.

He's going to do this again.

Her reverie was broken by the sound of Crivaro's voice.

"Come on, Riley. We're leaving."

She turned and saw that Crivaro and the sheriff were already stumbling out of the brush back onto the shoulder of the road.

"Quayle's driving us to the police station in town," Crivaro added.

Riley followed after them, and they all got into the sheriff's car.

As the sheriff drove away, Riley looked back at the cross the couple had just set up as a memorial to their dead daughter. Of course she'd seen hundreds of roadside shrines, but she'd always assumed they'd been set up as memorials of car accident victims.

It struck Riley as somehow strange to set up a shrine to mark the site of a hideous, grisly, premeditated crime.

No more crosses, she thought.

This has got to stop.

CHAPTER SEVEN

It wasn't the oncoming night that was making Riley feel uneasy. As Sheriff Quayle drove them into the small down of Dalhart, she eyed the rows of modest houses, some of them dark, and others with lighted windows. The houses were tidy, and the town looked perfectly comfortable and secure.

Riley was remembering something Claudia Dent had said about the murderer.

"Not somebody from around here. Somebody from elsewhere."

Riley didn't know whether to hope the woman was wrong or right. As far as Riley and Crivaro and the police were concerned, all that mattered was catching the killer as soon as possible.

But was that true for the Dents and all the other people who lived in this sleepy town? What if the killer turned out to be one of their own—maybe even a trusted friend, neighbor, and citizen? Would the town ever recover from the gnawing horror of such a shock?

They're going to have a hard time recovering one way or the other, Riley figured.

Still, she couldn't help thinking that the pain would run much deeper if the killer was someone who lived among them.

As they headed into town the town center, Sheriff Quayle pointed out a few of the local features, including a remarkably handsome courthouse, a brick building with white columns. Dalhart was the county seat, Quayle said.

As humble as it was, Riley sensed that the town gave off a certain aura of pride and prestige. The people who lived here considered themselves to be important—at least in the rural scheme of things.

Quayle parked outside the surprisingly large county law enforcement building, and Riley and Crivaro followed him on inside. The three of them sat down at a large table in a conference room.

Quayle said, "I want you to know that we've put out a public warning to all the towns in the area. Citizens have been notified that any missing persons should be reported immediately. And young women should not out walking alone, especially at night."

Quayle drummed his fingers on the table and added, "That's scarier to folks in these parts than people like you can probably imagine. The streets of Dalhart have always been as safe as can be, even at night. Women and girls could walk alone wherever they wanted, all hours. The same is true in Brattledale."

He inhaled and exhaled wearily.

"Times are really catching up with us, I guess," he said.

Crivaro asked, "Do you know when and where both girls were last seen before they disappeared?"

Quayle said, "In Brattledale, some of Natalie Booker's friends saw her leaving a weekly youth meeting at her church. Here in Dalhart, the last person to see Kimberly Dent was Goldie Dowling, the best friend Phil and Claudia mentioned."

Riley and Crivaro were both taking notes now.

Crivaro said, "I'm going to want to get in touch with Goldie ASAP— tonight if possible."

Quayle looked at his watch.

He said, "Isn't it getting kind of late for that kind of thing?"

Crivaro said, "I want to talk to her on the phone, at least. Her memories of last night are still fresh, and I don't want to wait until she starts forgetting things."

Quayle pushed a button on his intercom and asked for Goldie Dowling's phone number. He got his answer almost immediately.

Then Crivaro asked, "When did anybody notice that the girls were missing?"

Quayle said, "Well, Natalie's parents got worried when she didn't come home from church. They called the local police but the on-duty cops didn't take it seriously, thought it was just some typical rebellious teenage behavior. It wasn't the first time that local parents had called in about their kids not being home, only to have them turn up quickly. Those calls had never turned out to be anything before. The cops figured it was more of the same with Natalie."

Quayle shook his head.

"They should have known better, in Natalie's case," he said. "From what Sheriff Cole tells me, she was about as perfectly behaved as a small-town kid can be these days. She'd never have deliberately given her parents any cause for worry."

"What about Kimberly?" Riley asked.

Quayle said, "Her parents didn't notice she was missing until the next morning. They tend to go to bed early, and Kimberly would sometimes get home when they were already asleep. She'd come in quietly so she wouldn't wake them."

He asked, "How soon was Natalie's body found after she left the youth meeting?"

"Late the next day," Quayle said.

Crivaro looked at his notes and thumped his pencil eraser on the table.

He said, "So it sounds like we're looking at abductions that turned into murders. The van tracks at the crime scene are probably consistent with that. That kind of a vehicle would be useful for abducting a victim, then for transporting her after she was dead. Did either of the girls' bodies show signs of sexual abuse?"

"None whatsoever," Quayle said.

Crivaro sat silently for a few moments. Riley had some idea of what he might be thinking. The whole case might well hinge on what the perpetrator had been doing during the interval between the abductions and leaving the bodies. Had he intended to kill them from the start, or had something gone wrong to provoke him?

Then Crivaro said, "I want to take a look at the crime photos from both locations."

Quayle opened up a folder and spread several pictures across the table.

Riley felt an unexpected jolt of horror.

She was shocked at her own reaction. She'd seen dead bodies before—in real life, not just in photographs. And she'd seen them in far more shocking conditions than these bodies, which showed no signs of violence except for strangulation marks on their necks.

Why is this hitting me so hard? she wondered.

Crivaro and Quayle kept talking, but Riley felt as though their voices were getting farther and farther away, and that she was all alone with these troubling images.

Both girls were carefully laid out on the ground, perfectly straight and with their hands crossed on their chests.

Almost like in a coffin, she thought.

She remembered the impression she'd gotten of the killer at the crime scene—that he'd felt no anger or hostility toward his victims.

What she saw now all but proved that impression. The killer had taken great care in how he'd treated these girls' bodies, making sure that they'd be found in as dignified a condition as he could manage.

Riley was flooded with alarm now.

The air felt too thick to breathe.

She leapt to her feet and blurted, "Excuse me."

Then she rushed out of the room and all the way outside the building. The cold air came as a sharp relief, and she could breathe again. But it was all she could do to keep from hyperventilating.

What's wrong with me? she thought.

She closed her eyes, and an image came to her sharp and clear. It was Heidi Wright again, staring into that snowfall as her body lay crumpled and dying on the parking lot pavement. Blood was gushing out of her chest onto the fallen snow, and her mouth was working silently as she breathed her last breaths.

Then she fell still, and her dead eyes kept staring into space with an expression of deep sadness.

Riley was shaking all over now.

Natalie and Kimberly had been slightly older than Heidi. But having lived more sheltered and innocent lives, they'd actually seemed younger. The three girls suddenly seemed very much alike. And a terrible question lurked at the edges of Riley's mind.

It was a crazy, preposterous question, and she tried to fight it down, to keep it from surfacing into her consciousness.

But the question finally broke through, and Riley whispered it aloud.

"Am I just like the killer?"

Riley shuddered with a violent spasm.

No, of course not!

How could she even consider it? Heidi had been pointing a gun at Riley, threatening her life. If Riley hadn't fired, she herself would be dead now. So why on earth was she likening herself to the killer, who had taken two perfectly innocent lives?

Riley sat down on a cold, concrete bench outside the police station. She thought back to the photos she'd just seen of the two dead girls. Their expressions had been so different from Heidi's when she had died—as calm and tranquil as if they were asleep, not dead.

He took such care with them, Riley thought.

He hadn't just thrown them aside after he'd killed them, dumping them in a ditch somewhere. He'd treated their bodies with respect and even honor. But the last time Riley had seen Heidi, she'd still been crumpled grotesquely on that pavement. Riley had done nothing to change that.

Riley struggled to bring her shaking under control.

Crazy thoughts, she told herself.

None of it made any sense and she knew it. What was she supposed to do after she'd shot and killed Heidi? Stretch her out nicely and cross her arms over her chest and close her eyes? She couldn't have done those things even if she'd wanted to—not right there at the crime scene.

And yet . . .

But no, there was no "and yet" about it. Riley hadn't done anything wrong. Everyone kept telling her that. She'd done everything by the book. She couldn't have done it any other way.

As her body and her nerves started to settle down and she began to breathe more easily, she remembered how she'd rushed out of the conference room just now. She felt a flush of embarrassment and shame.

What must Sheriff Quayle think of me?

For that matter, what must Crivaro have thought of her? In a fit of panic, she'd walked out on her partner without warning, right in the middle of an urgent meeting. How could she explain her behavior to him when she barely understood it herself? An apology seemed hardly sufficient.

I've got to go back in there, she thought.

But she couldn't—not yet, not until she felt sure she wasn't going to fall apart all over again. She decided to give herself a few more minutes to pull herself together.

She sighed deeply as she remembered Crivaro's warning over the phone.

"You need to get some counseling under your belt before you come back to work."

But she'd ignored his warning and insisted on coming to work with him anyway. Had that been an awful mistake? Was she in any condition to solve a case like this one—a case in which the victims themselves reminded her of a girl she'd killed just yesterday? Riley's confidence was badly shaken.

But I've got to try, she thought.

More than that, she knew she had to succeed.

Other innocent lives might yet be at stake.

CHAPTER EIGHT

Jake Crivaro sat staring at the open doorway.

What got into Riley? he wondered. Jake's young partner had just rushed out into the hall in the middle of their examination of photos from two murders. He glanced at Sheriff Quayle and saw that the local lawman looked as puzzled as Jake felt.

Quayle got up from his chair and walked over to the open door. He peered out into the hallway, then shook his head.

As he pulled the door shut, Quayle asked Jake, "What was that all about?"

Jake felt stymied. He didn't want the sheriff to think Riley got squeamish at the sight of corpses—and just photos of corpses at that. Jake himself knew Riley much too well to think any such thing, but at the moment he wasn't sure what was going on.

"She'll be all right," Jake replied, trying to sound more certain than he felt..

It seemed like a lame answer, but Jake figured it would have to do. He just hoped that he hadn't made a mistake bringing Riley along on this case so soon after the last one. If necessary, he'd send her back to Quantico, but he knew that wouldn't look good on her records. Besides, Lehl might send him some other partner who'd turn out to be a pain in the ass.

With a skeptical look, Sheriff Quayle took his seat again.

When Jake turned back to the photos on the table, he suddenly felt as though he understood. The faces of these young murdered girls had reminded Riley of Heidi Wright.

Jake's heart went out to Riley.

The poor kid. It must have come as a shock.

She'd probably just had to go outside to get some fresh air. But how could he explain to Quayle what Riley was going through?

43

Jake looked at his watch and said, "If I'm going to talk to Kimberly's friend, I'd better do it right now."

Sheriff Quayle nodded and said, "I'll see if they're at home."

Quayle punched in the number on the desk phone. Then from what Quayle was saying, the girl's mother must have answered.

"Jean, this is Ed Quayle, over at the police station. I'm sorry to bother you at this hour. But a couple of FBI agents flew in from Quantico to help on—you know, the awful things that have happened. One of the agents wants to talk to Goldie. I was wondering . . . we could come right on over . . ."

He fell quiet as he listened to the mother's reply. Jake immediately sensed that she was putting up some resistance.

Then Quayle said, "I understand, Jean. But Agent Crivaro thinks she might be able to help. He'd like to talk to her right away if he possibly can. I'm sure you can understand how urgent this is. We've got to move as quickly as we can."

Quayle paused again, then said, "Thanks, Jean."

When he turned to back to Jake, his previous demeanor kicked back in. "Okay, let's get on over there. But don't you guys go making things any worse than you have to. These are good people."

Jake just nodded. He was becoming a little amused by the sheriff's shifting attitudes.

As he followed Quayle through the hallway, he looked for Riley, but didn't see her anywhere. He thought maybe he should have someone check the ladies' room, but Quayle was moving toward the front door, obviously not waiting for anyone.

As they stepped out the door, he was about to ask Quayle to hold up for a minute. Then, to his relief, he saw Riley right there outside, standing in front of the building. He thought she looked less queasy than when she'd rushed out of the room

Jake said to her, "Quayle has set up a meeting with Kimberly's friend. We're going there now"

Riley nodded and followed along behind them. Without a word, she climbed into the back of Quayle's police car and Jake took the passenger's seat.

It was just a short drive to the Dowlings' house, a simple bungalow that looked much like all the others on the streets they passed through. A woman in her forties let them inside, looking anxious and worried.

After they were all in the living room, the mother called out, "Goldie, the people I told you about are here."

The teenager came slowly into the room. Her hair, clearly the source of her nickname, was in disarray, and her eyes were red.

Quayle said, "Hey, Goldie. How are you holding up?"

"Okay I guess, Sheriff Ed," she replied, managing a weak smile.

Jake was rather intrigued.

Sheriff Ed?

That must be what kids called him here in Dalhart.

The girl sat down on one end of a well-used sofa and the sheriff sat beside her.

"Yeah, I know, it's rough, kid," Quayle said. "It's hard on all of us, but I know it's especially hard on you. But you keep hanging in there, okay? Someday all this will seem like it happened a long, long time ago."

Goldie glanced over at Jake and Riley, who were still standing.

"Listen, Goldie," Quayle said, "your mom may have told you I've got a couple of BAU agents from the FBI here on this case. We really need their help to find whoever did this to Kimberly. The agents want to talk to you right now, if that's okay. Their names are Agents Crivaro and Sweeney. Agent Sweeney is a nice young lady."

Jake still wasn't used to this gentler side of Quayle but he realized that the lawman must have a remarkable rapport with the kids in town.

I guess that's one good reason he's sheriff, he thought.

Although Quayle worked in law enforcement like Jake did, their jobs couldn't be more different. Jake wondered how it might feel to serve a single community instead of darting around the country all the time.

Very comfortable for the right kind of guy, he thought. Jake somehow doubted that he himself was temperamentally suited for it.

Goldie glanced up at Jake and Riley again, then muttered, "Okay."

Quayle said "Thanks, Goldie."

He got up from the sofa, and Riley sat down in his place. Jake sat in a chair facing Riley and Goldie.

Sheriff Quayle walked to the other side of the small room, where Goldie's mother was standing, looking agitated. Jake was pleased when he saw the sheriff engage the woman in conversation and lead her a little farther away from the interview.

Trying to sound unofficial and unintimidating, Jake said, "I'm sorry to have to bother you at such a terrible time."

"It's okay," the girl said in a shaky voice.

Jake said, "I understand that you were the last person to see Kimberly last night."

"Yeah, she was visiting me at my house."

"Did she visit you often at night?" Jake asked.

"Yeah, kind of a lot, I guess."

Goldie choked slightly and added, "She was my best friend."

Jake could see that his young partner was looking almost as distressed as the teenager he was questioning.

"I'm sorry," Jake told Goldie again. "Did other people know you spent evenings together?"

"Yeah, I suppose so. We talked about it with friends, I guess. It wasn't like it was a secret or anything. Lots of kids do the same thing—just hanging out at night, you know?"

"I understand," Jake said. "Was there anything different about last night's visit?"

"She stayed later than usual, I guess. She left around midnight, I think."

Then the girl added in a choked voice, "I keep thinking this was maybe my fault. Should I have walked home with her? Would that have made a difference?"

Jake fought down a discouraged sigh. Comforting interviewees in their guilt wasn't one of his strong points.

He was relieved when Riley spoke up with a fairly steady voice.

"Goldie, it's normal to feel this way, but you've got to believe this wasn't your fault. You and Kimberly had no reason to think last night was different from any other night. There's only one person whose fault this is, and my partner and I are going to do everything we can to bring him to justice."

"Okay," Goldie whispered.

Jake thought for a moment, then said, "Goldie, maybe you heard about something similar happening to a girl in Brattledale. Her name was Natalie Booker. Did you and Kimberly happen to know her?"

Goldie said, "I didn't, and I don't think Kimberly did either. Actually, I don't remember hearing her name until... what happened to her. Kimberly and I didn't spend any time over in Brattledale."

Jake shifted restlessly in his chair. It might make it a lot easier to solve the case if the two victims had been connected in some way. But so far, he had no reason to think they knew each other at all.

He said, "Do you know anybody who might have meant Kimberly any harm?"

"Oh, no. Everybody liked her."

"Are you sure?" Jake asked. "Was there anybody she wasn't getting along with during the last week or so, even if it wasn't about anything important?"

Goldie fell silent for a moment.

"No, I don't think so," Goldie said.

Jake felt a tingle of suspicion.

She's not telling the truth, he thought.

Riley apparently felt the same way. She said, "Goldie, you've got to tell us everything."

Another silence fell.

Sheriff Quayle stepped back from across the room and spoke up, sounding warmer and kinder than even before.

"Goldie, you and I have known each other all your life. You know you can trust me. And you know you can believe me when I say you can trust Agents Crivaro and Sweeney. We're not trying to pry. We only care about one thing, and that's finding whoever did this to Kimberly. If you know anything, you really have to tell us."

Yet another silence fell.

Quayle sat down on the sofa again, taking the space between Riley and Goldie. He just waited quietly.

Then Goldie said, "Kimberly really didn't want her parents to find out. You've got to promise not to tell them."

Quayle shook his head. "I'm sorry, Goldie, but I can't promise anything like that. All I can say is that the time for keeping secrets from *anybody* is over. Think about Kimberly's parents. Do you really think they'd be angry with her *now* about whatever it is she didn't want them to know?"

There was another pause.

Then Goldie said, "Kimberly's parents were really strict with her—about boys and dating and all that kind of thing. They were very old-fashioned. I thought it was kind of weird. It was like, if a guy so much as kissed her, they might think she should get married or at least engaged or something. So she didn't want them to know that she was going out with somebody."

"Who was it, Goldie?" Quayle asked.

"Jay Napier," Goldie said.

Quayle nodded. Jake could tell the name was familiar to him.

Quayle asked, "Was she having any troubles with Jay recently?"

"Kind of," Goldie said. "Jay broke up with her. And he was being kind of a jerk about it."

"How so?" Riley asked.

"Well, he was going around bad-mouthing her—to other boys at school, anyway. He started telling them..."

Her voice faded for a moment, then she said, "Look, Jay got kind of pushy with her. He wanted... well, let's just say Kimberly didn't feel ready for—what he wanted. So he broke up with her, and started telling all the guys why he'd broken up with her. It really upset her."

Riley asked, "Did Jay do anything else that upset her?"

"He started following her around a lot, pestering her."

"Stalking her, you mean?" Riley asked.

"Kind of, yeah. Or maybe not stalking exactly... Look, maybe I shouldn't have said anything. I don't think it was all that serious. I mean, I don't think Jay would really have done anything like..."

Her voice faded away again.

Sheriff Quayle said, "You were right to tell us, Goldie. We've got to know as much as possible about whatever was going on with Kimberly recently. We can't ignore anything at all."

Jake added, "You've been a great help, Goldie."

Then the girl let out a choked sob.

"I miss her so much," Goldie said, crying now.

"I know you do," Sheriff Quayle said, his own voice thick with emotion. "She was your best friend, and you miss her even more than most of us do. We've all just got to do everything we can to make things right for her. And we've got to make sure this doesn't happen to anybody else."

"I know," Goldie said.

"Thank you for being honest with us," Quayle said.

"Can I go now?" Goldie pleaded.

"Of course you can," Quayle told her. "You've been a real help."

"Thank you," Goldie whispered as she got up and scurried out of the room.

The two agents got to their feet, and Quayle did too. The sheriff stepped aside and spoke to Goldie's mother, thanking her for letting them come and praising her daughter for her bravery and honesty. He also said he knew they'd upset Goldie, and he told her she should spend a little time with her daughter right now to make her feel better.

When they were back in the police car, Jake asked, "Do you know this boy Goldie mentioned—Jay Napier?"

Quayle nodded and said, "Yeah, I've known him all his life."

Riley asked, "Do you think he's capable of murder?"

Quayle squinted thoughtfully.

"The truth is, I really don't know," he said. "He was just a regular kid growing up—nothing exceptional or unusual about him. But he's changed some during the last couple of years, since his parents' marriage broke up. It's not like he's done anything really bad—certainly nothing criminal, but..."

Quayle was quiet for a moment.

Then he said, "It's just his general attitude, I guess. He's not as polite as he used to be. He's gotten to be kind of... well, snotty, you might say, especially toward adults. And I've heard that he hasn't treated some other girls he's dated very nicely."

"Has he been violent toward them?" Riley asked.

"No, nothing like that, or at least nothing I've heard of. He's just... well, like Goldie just said, pushy."

Quayle drummed his fingers on the steering wheel and added, "I guess we'd better talk to the kid. We can't leave any stone unturned, can we? As it happens, he should be pretty easy to reach. He works nights right near the police station at the local Tobin's fast food joint. He's probably there right now."

The sheriff drove back to the station. After he parked the car and they all got out he said, "Let's walk over to Tobin's and pay the kid a visit." Then something else occurred to him and he pulled out his phone and alerted one of his cops to get a vehicle ready for the agents' use while they were here in Dalhart. He also told the cop to call and make a reservation for Riley and Jake at a local motel. Then he added grumpily, "If we've got to have folks like this around here, we might as make things convenient for them."

Jake almost laughed aloud to hear the sheriff revert to his sterner persona. Any traces of the fatherly "Sheriff Ed" vanished now that he was dealing with two FBI agents and not regular townspeople.

As they walked toward short distance to the fast food place, Jake looked at his young partner. She still seemed agitated.

He asked, "Are you okay, Riley?"

Riley looked at him as if she were surprised to see him walking beside her. She said, "Yeah, I'm ... I'll be okay. I'll be just fine."

Jake didn't like the note of uncertainty in her voice.

She's not fine, he thought. *She's a long way from fine.*

CHAPTER NINE

As she and Agent Crivaro followed Sheriff Quayle toward the fast food place, Riley winced with embarrassment.

Crivaro had just asked...

"Are you okay, Riley?"

She hated that he'd felt the need to ask her that question.

Even more, she hated that she wasn't sure how to answer it.

Am I okay?

Am I going to be okay?

After all her early experiences, her training at the Academy, and working on three murder cases since her graduation, Riley could hardly believe she'd been so badly shaken by a few photographs. She had confronted real flesh-and-blood horrors and was likely to be faced with more of them before this case was over.

The question still hovered in her mind.

Am I really up to it?

She knew she'd better decide one way or the other, and do it quickly. If she didn't think she could do the job, Agent Crivaro deserved to know right now. It would be terrible to fall apart on him in the middle of a case.

Riley was still struggling to make up her mind when she, Crivaro, and Sheriff Quayle reached their destination. Tobin's fast food place gleamed brightly in the midst of the dark, cold, quiet neighborhood.

She could see through the enormous plate glass windows that there wasn't a single customer inside. She wondered whether a fast food place got enough business on a weekday night in a small town like this to be really worth keeping it open.

Before they went inside, Crivaro asked Quayle to say as little as possible during the interview, and to leave the questioning to himself and Riley.

51

The sheriff scowled, but then he nodded glumly.

Riley and her two colleagues walked into the sparkling interior. Riley and Crivaro sat down at a table while Sheriff Quayle went up to the counter to ask if Jay Napier could take a break from work.

Soon Quayle came over to their table, followed by a teenaged boy who was wearing a Tobin's uniform and an apron. Quayle was carrying a stack of cards in his hands. They looked like an employee's time cards.

Riley saw that the boy was slightly above medium height and quite muscular. She figured he was quite capable of killing—physically, at least.

The sheriff and the boy sat down across from Riley and Crivaro. When Quayle made the necessary introductions, and the boy's eyes widened expectantly.

"So you're from the FBI, huh?" he said to Riley and Crivaro. "The BAU, even! Wow! What do you want to talk to me about?"

Crivaro said, "We'd like to talk to you about Kimberly Dent."

"The girl who got killed, you mean," Jay said with a shrug. "Yeah, it was awful what happened to her. But what does it have to do with me?"

Crivaro stared at him intently and said, "Well, Jay, we're kind of hoping you can answer that question for us."

Jay chuckled nervously.

He said, "Um, I guess I don't know what you mean."

Riley felt a tingle of interest.

He's evading already, she thought.

She also noticed something odd about the boy's expression. He didn't seem to have stopped smiling since he'd sat down with them. She remembered what Quayle had told them back at the station about his "snotty" attitude.

Is he smirking at us? Riley wondered. *Does he think he's putting something over on use? Or is it a smile?*

Maybe that slightly smug and insolent expression was natural for him—even habitual. Riley knew that his face was going to be unusually hard to read for honesty or dishonesty.

Crivaro said, "What can you tell us about her?"

Jay's eyes darted back and forth between Crivaro and Riley.

"I dunno," he said. "What do you want me to tell you?"

Crivaro didn't answer, and Riley thought she understood his tactic. If Jay was in any way guilty, the best way to find out was to let him trap himself in his own attempted deceptions. Riley just hoped Sheriff Quayle did as he was told and didn't interrupt with thoughts and questions of his own.

After an awkward silence, Jay said, "She was a nice girl, I guess. She didn't deserve what happened to her. What else do you want me to say?"

Crivaro shrugged and said, "What do you want to tell us?"

"She was a nice girl," Jay repeated. "I can't say I knew her all that well."

Crivaro pointed a finger at Jay and spoke sharply.

"Kid, don't play games with me. I know kids your age inside and out. I can smell when you're lying a mile away. Isn't it bad enough that an innocent girl is dead? And now you're going to lie about her?"

Riley was startled. Crivaro suddenly sounded a lot more like a scolding father than an FBI agent.

Jay recoiled as if he'd been slapped.

Then he said, "Okay, we'd been dating."

"Why didn't you tell us so in the first place?" Crivaro said.

"You didn't ask," the boy said, sounding a little frightened now.

Crivaro said, "Yeah, we pretty much did. Or are you really stupid, so you need me to spell out in big letters that we want the whole truth from you? You told us you didn't know her all that well."

Jay shrugged and said, "Well, I didn't lie."

"It's a lie the way I see it," Crivaro said. "And in case you didn't know, it's against the law to lie to a federal law enforcement officer."

Although that smirk-like twist remained on Jay's lips, his eyes registered some alarm.

He said, "Look, sometimes you think you know someone and you find out you really don't. You know what I mean?"

"No, we don't," Riley put in. "Please explain."

"You'll need to go into more detail," Crivaro added.

Jay sighed and said, "So, Kimberly and I grew up together, and after a lot of years we got interested in each other and started dating, but I guess we weren't exactly what each other expected after all, so she broke up with me."

Crivaro grunted with annoyance.

"Aw, come on, kid," Crivaro said. "Do you really think we don't know any better than that?"

Jay's eyes darted around.

"How am I supposed to know what you already know?" he said.

"You can't," Riley said. "That's kind of the point." Now she had to stop herself from smirking.

Jay said, "Who have you been talking to about me, anyway? Did you talk to Goldie Dowling? Because she's liable to badmouth me. Don't believe anything she told you."

"Who said we talked to anybody about you?" Crivaro said. "All we want to know is, who broke up with who, and why?"

Jay let out a discouraged groan and said, "Okay, I broke up with her. Things weren't working out the way I hoped."

"And how was that?" Crivaro asked.

Jay rolled his eyes.

"I dunno, they just didn't," he said.

Crivaro snorted. "She wouldn't put out, huh?"

"I didn't say that," Jay said.

"Yeah, but that's always the reason, isn't it?" Crivaro said, sounding again like a strict father. "Don't try to fool me, kid. I used to have teenage hormones myself, you know. I know what it's like."

"She just wasn't interested in taking the next step, that's all," he said.

"You mean sex," Riley said.

"Yeah, that's what I mean," Jay said. "Look, I wasn't looking for some one-time thing. I wanted a relationship. I hoped we'd get married someday."

He looked out the window with wistful eyes.

He said, "You've got no idea what life is like in a town like this—especially when you know it's a dead end, and you're going to wind up spending your whole life here, settling down to some shit job forever. I just got desperate for something real, something to look forward to. But with her, everything was...well, it was like we were still in grade school or something. She didn't treat it—*us*—like we meant anything."

He suddenly sounded perfectly sincere to Riley. And yet she still saw that odd twist at the edges of his lips.

Is this just an act? she wondered.

Everything about his demeanor told her he meant every word of what he was saying—except for that strange half-smile.

Crivaro said, "And after it was over, you went around telling everybody—what?"

Jay's voice dropped to a near-whisper.

"I didn't tell anybody anything."

"No?" said Riley. "You didn't go around telling your guy friends she was some kind of tease? And you didn't follow her around making a nuisance of yourself after you ended it?"

Jay slapped his hand against the table.

"I didn't kill her!" he said. "That's what this is all about, isn't it? I'd never do anything like that to anybody."

Crivaro said, "So where were you the night before last?"

"I was right here working," Jay said.

Sheriff Quayle had been dutifully quiet so far. But Riley noticed that he'd been studying the time cards while they'd been talking. She figured now was a good time to bring him into the conversation.

"Is he telling the truth?" she asked Sheriff Quayle.

"He was working that night," Quayle said. "He clocked out at 12:45."

"That's right," Jay said. "We close at midnight, but I've got to stay awhile after that to break things down."

Riley and Crivaro exchanged glances. She knew that she and her partner were thinking the same thing.

Goldie said Kimberly left her house around midnight.

But the girl hadn't sounded at all certain about the time. If Kimberly had ended her visit later than Goldie had thought, Jay might still have caught up with her as she walked home, especially if he knew when and where to expect her. The punched time card was hardly any kind of alibi.

Crivaro drummed his fingers on the table.

He said to Jay, "What about Wednesday night, exactly a week ago?"

"What about it?" Jay said, with a note of sourness in his voice.

"Where were you?" Crivaro asked.

"I dunno," Jay said. "Here working, I guess."

Looking at the cards, Sheriff Quayle shook his head and said, "Huh-uh. You didn't work that night at all."

Jay threw his hands up in the air.

"Okay, so I forgot, and I don't know what the hell I was doing that night," he said. "What's this got to do with anything, anyway?"

"Have you got a car, Jay?" Riley asked.

"Yeah, so what?" Jay said.

"Do you ever drive over to Brattledale?" Riley asked.

Jay's eyes widened.

He said, "Are you asking me about the other girl now? The girl who was killed over in Brattledale? Her name was Natalie something, right? I sure as hell didn't kill her. I never even knew her."

"So where were you that night, then?" Crivaro asked.

Jay seemed to think for a moment.

Then he said, "I was with my pals over at Fritz Montag's house. We were there way into the morning hours, playing music."

"Music?" Riley said.

"Yeah, we've all got instruments, and we get together and jam when we can. We suck too much to play in public, but when we hang out over at Fritz's, we get to pretend we're rock and roll stars. You can check with Fritz and any of the guys—Lou, Leroy, and Mitch."

Sheriff Quayle said, "I'll get in touch with all of them."

"You do that," Jay said irritably. "Better yet, call Fritz's parents. They were really pissed off because we kept them awake half the night. They'll tell you I was there."

Jay got up from his seat and said, "If there's nothing else, I need to get back to work.

"Hold on just a minute," Quayle said as the boy started to walk away.

"Leave him alone," Crivaro said. "That's all we're going to get out of him for now."

Riley watched as Jay went back behind the counter. Then he turned and looked straight at her. And again, she noticed that strange, smirking expression that had never left his lips since she'd first met him. She knew that it might just be his normal expression, something he couldn't even help.

But she couldn't be sure, and she found herself wondering—was Jay Napier just some innocent high school kid?

Or was he a sociopathic monster?

CHAPTER TEN

As Jay Napier disappeared back into the kitchen area of the fast food restaurant, Riley knew she wasn't the only person sitting at that table wondering about him. Was this insolent boy guilty or innocent?

At this point, she didn't know, but someone needed to find out.

Sheriff Quayle drummed his fingers on the plastic tabletop.

He asked, "So what do you Feds think of the kid?"

Crivaro tilted his head and said, "Well, we don't have anything to bring him in on—at least not yet. You'd better check out his alibi for the killing in Brattledale. And quickly, too, before he can get his pals to coordinate their stories."

"I'll call the Montags right away," Quayle said.

Crivaro added, "And have one of your night duty guys watch his movements tonight. Keep watching him tomorrow, too. He might be a flight risk. Of course, if his alibi for Brattledale holds up, you can skip all that stuff. If he didn't kill the girl there, we can be all but sure he didn't kill Kimberly Dent, either."

"Got it," Quayle said, rising from the table. "You two must be hungry. This is the only food joint that's open in Dalhart at this hour, so you might want to grab something while you're here. I'll send one of my boys by here with a car you can use, and he'll tell you how to get to your motel."

Quayle looked over toward the kitchen area and sighed bitterly.

He said, "I never thought I'd see the day when we couldn't trust our own in this town."

Then he glowered at Riley and Crivaro.

"I'll sure as hell be glad to see the last of you two," he said.

He walked out into the night without another word. Riley stared after him with surprise. Then she remembered how the sheriff had seemed to dislike her and Crivaro from the moment he'd set eyes on them.

"What's with that guy?" she murmured to Crivaro. "What does he have against us?"

"It's something you're liable to run into from time to time," Crivaro said. "We federal agents aren't always welcome guests—especially in rural areas like this."

"But he asked for the BAU's help," Riley said.

"Yeah, because he knew he really needed it," Crivaro said. "And that irritates him all the more. We represent everything these small town folks fear and mistrust and downright loathe. We're big city, big government, big law enforcement—big everything. They don't like us. They like life to stay small."

Crivaro shrugged and added, "Sometimes it's almost like these local cops blame us for the cases we're here to solve—as if we're accomplices somehow. It's not fair, and it might even seem kind of stupid, but there it is."

Riley shook her head and said, "It's going to take some getting used to."

"Yeah, there's a lot about this job that takes getting used to," Crivaro said.

Riley noticed an odd note of irritably in his voice, as if he was leaving something unpleasant unsaid.

Crivaro stared out the window for a moment.

Then he said, "What do you think about the kid we just talked to?"

"I don't know," Riley said. "I had trouble reading him. Something about his face."

"I know what you mean," Crivaro said. "He's got one of those expressions that are kind of hard to read. You'll run into those from time to time."

Riley chuckled and said, "Well, you sure shook him up when he tried to lie to you about his relationship with the girl. You really went all papa bear on him, like a dad reading a teenage kid the riot act. I've never seen you get into that mode before."

Crivaro growled under his breath.

"Yeah, well, I've had some experience along those lines. I raised a son, remember? Getting him through adolescence was murder. It toughened me up more than a lot of murder cases. Come on, let's get something to eat."

As they walked toward the counter, Riley was surprised at what Crivaro had just said. The only other time he'd ever mentioned having a son was once when he'd warned her about the havoc being a BAU agent could wreak on her personal life.

"It gets hard to just be a human being," he'd told her.

She knew that his divorce and his estranged son were sensitive subjects that he didn't like to talk about.

At the counter she and Crivaro ordered some burgers from a girl who looked extremely curious about them. Riley could understand why. It wasn't every day when a Tobin's employee got questioned by the authorities. Riley could see Jay peeking warily at them through some shelves that separated the kitchen from the front counter. She wished she had a better idea of what to think of him.

When they got their burgers and went back to their table, Riley knew it was time to bring up a subject she'd much rather put behind her.

She said, "Agent Crivaro, about what happened earlier, back at the station—"

Crivaro interrupted, "It can't happen again, Riley."

Riley was startled by the sharpness in his voice.

He took a bite of his burger and said, "Look, I get it. We've got two teenage victims—sweet-faced, innocent-looking girls. They remind you of Heidi Wright. Their photos triggered your trauma. But I can't have you running out on meetings like that—especially when we're working with a guy as prickly as Sheriff Quayle. It just can't happen."

Riley sat staring at him for a moment.

Crivaro said, "We talked about all this earlier. You can't expect me to understand what you're going through. My own first experience with deadly force wasn't anything like yours. I can't be your therapist and your partner at the same time. In fact, I've got no business being your therapist at all."

"I understand," Riley whispered.

"Do you?" Crivaro said.

He held her gaze for a long moment.

Then he said, "We've both got a decision to make, right here and now. If you don't think you can do this, that's fine, I won't hold it against you, and no one else will either. I can ask for another partner for this case, or I can work it on my own. It's no problem for me either way. Meanwhile, you can see that therapist, and after you get your head straight, I'll be glad to work with you again. Is that what you want?"

Riley felt positively stricken.

She remembered her own doubts of a little while ago.

"Are you okay, Riley?" Crivaro had asked when they'd been walking here. Again she wondered . . .

Am I okay?

Am I going to be okay?

Riley felt a lump of emotion in her throat.

Don't cry, she told herself.

That would be the worst thing she could do right now.

It might even be the end of her BAU career.

"I can do this," she finally said in as firm a voice as she could muster.

"Are you sure?" Crivaro asked.

"I'm sure," Riley said.

"Okay," Crivaro said, taking another bite of his burger.

The truth was, Riley didn't feel sure of it at all. She only knew that she couldn't bring herself to give up on a case right now. She especially didn't want to fail because her emotions were getting the best of her.

I want to be better than that, she thought.

I've got to be better than that.

Just as they were finishing their burgers, Crivaro's phone rang. As Riley listened to Crivaro's monosyllabic replies, she realized the call was from Sheriff Quayle.

Crivaro ended the call and put the phone back in his pocket.

He frowned and said, "Jay Napier's alibi holds up. Quayle called the house where Jay and his pals were supposed to be jamming that night. The parents there confirmed it. So did some of Jay's friends when he called them."

"Should we tell Jay?" Riley said.

"No, the sheriff's going to call him here and tell him personally."

Riley fought down a discouraged sigh. She'd really hoped that Jay would prove to be their killer, and they could put an end to these murders once and for all.

Just then a car pulled up and parked in the restaurant parking lot. A uniformed cop got out and came inside.

He called out to Riley and Crivaro, "I've got a car you guys can use. I'll tell you how to get to your motel."

Riley and Crivaro put their paper cups and wrappers in the trash. Before they followed the cop out the door, Riley glanced back toward the counter.

Once again, she could see Jay's face among the shelves, peeking out from the kitchen area. She couldn't see his lips, but she felt pretty sure that half-smile was there.

Just habitual, I guess, she thought.

It bothered her that she hadn't been able to read him at all, despite the instincts she'd gotten so much praise and attention for.

Some instincts, she thought as she and Crivaro walked outside to the waiting vehicle and started to drive to their motel.

An eerie feeling of déjà vu came over Riley when she opened her motel room door and walked inside. She wondered—what was it about this room that seemed so familiar to her?

Then it dawned on her.

Everything about it seems familiar.

She'd stayed in several motels since she'd started working on murder cases with Jake Crivaro last year. It hadn't occurred to her until just now that they were all strangely identical.

The decor was different, of course. This room had a divider and wallpaper with star motifs, while the room she had stayed in during their case in Maryland was leaf-themed, and an earlier room in West Virginia had diamond patterns everywhere.

But all the rooms had been about the same size, with two twin beds, a table between them, the same number of lamps, and the same number of paintings of similar sizes hanging in nearly the same positions on the walls.

It was as if somebody kept moving the same room around wherever Riley went, applying different decor in order to fool her into thinking she was actually in different places.

She didn't believe it, of course. But she was tired, and her mind was playing tricks on her. Today had been a long, difficult day, and just yesterday she had killed another human being for the first time. But what was it about the similarities among the motel rooms that troubled her?

As she stretched out on one of the beds, a word popped into her mind.

Monotony.

Was that it? Was she maybe getting a hint that her life as a BAU agent was going to become monotonous, even achingly repetitious?

How could that be possible? she wondered.

In just a few short months, she'd helped to thwart a bizarre assortment of killers—a twisted college professor who murdered students in the interest of "research," a crazed clown who injected his victims with fatal doses of amphetamine, a monster who wrapped his victims in barbed wire, another who slashed women's throats and left their bodies to the elements...

Even so, she couldn't help but wonder—might all evil be the same deep down? Were the very killers she pursued somehow as much alike as these motel rooms? If so, would she someday become numb to the horrors she would face time and time again?

She shuddered at the thought.

Maybe it was better to feel traumatized than to feel numb.

She sighed and tried to persuade herself to get up from the bed, get out of the clothes she'd been wearing all day, and climb under the covers for a serious night's sleep.

But she felt too tired to move.

She took her cellphone out of her pocket and checked it for messages. There were none—not even from Ryan, who was probably getting ready for bed himself right about now.

She wondered how his day had been. What had he been doing at the law firm today? What time had he gotten back to their apartment? What had he eaten for dinner in her absence? And most of all—did he miss her?

I should call him, she thought.

But somehow, she couldn't make herself do it.

She remembered their difficult phone conversation this morning.

"I don't want you to go," he'd said.

And she couldn't blame him for his disappointment. He'd had a romantic evening planned at their favorite restaurant. And after it was over, he'd hoped to come home and restore some of the intimacy they seemed to have lost since she'd become involved with the FBI.

She remembered the sad tone in his voice when he'd broached the subject.

"It's been a long time since we ... you know."

She thought about how different things would be right now if she'd simply told Crivaro that she couldn't take this case. He'd given her every opportunity to say no. If she had, she and Ryan might be making love right now.

Wouldn't that be better than lying here alone?

Why *had* she chosen as she did? Was it possible that she was trying to push Ryan away? Was she actually trying to avoid restoring the intimacy that had been slipping away between them? Did she somehow feel more at home in bland, indistinguishable motel rooms like this than she did in the apartment where they were trying to make a life together?

She didn't know, but she felt pretty sure of one thing.

I've got to talk to that therapist.

She forced herself to get up and go to the bathroom and get ready for bed. When she lay back down under the covers, she wondered—what was this new case going to be like? How was it going to feel to track down a new killer?

And was she going to have to take another life?

As she faded off to sleep, she remembered the photos of those innocent, murdered girls. If she had to kill the monster who had taken their lives, surely she wouldn't feel bad about it this time.

Maybe I'll even like it, she thought.

CHAPTER ELEVEN

The only thing Sandra knew at first was that everything was dark. Then the pain set in—the worst headache she could ever remember. She dimly realized that she was lying on a hard, cold surface in total darkness.

But where am I? she wondered.

She tried to move, to sit up, but something was restraining her arms. Her wrists were bound together. Then she tried to move her legs, but her ankles were held fast.

Sandra forced down the panic she felt rising. She struggled to think calmly and clearly.

How did I get here?

She realized she must have been unconscious and was just starting to come to again. Then she gasped as a vague memory surfaced...

She'd been struck. She'd been knocked out. She strained to remember how and when, but it was hard to think over the pounding pain in her head.

I've got to remember, she told herself.

The only thing Sandra felt sure of was that she was in terrible danger. How could she get out of this situation if she had no idea what had happened in the first place?

Slowly, bits and pieces began to come back to her.

She'd been out walking on the school grounds as she often did at night when she had trouble sleeping. She vaguely remembered Sister Agnes putting out some kind of warning for everybody to stay indoors that night, but Sandra had ignored it. The idea that there could be any danger on those grounds had seemed silly to her. It had been cold outside, but she enjoyed the bracing chill in the air.

Then she'd seen a vehicle of some sort.

Yes, a van.

It had been parked ahead on the wide campus sidewalk where she was walking. She remembered feeling angry for a moment. The school was constantly trying to keep people from parking or standing their cars on those pavements. But she'd told herself not to be angry.

I mustn't judge, lest I be judged, she'd thought.

Whoever had parked there at this time of night probably didn't know the campus rules. The van's engine had been running, so the driver must have stopped there for some understandable reason—engine trouble, perhaps or to look at a map for directions.

Maybe I can help, she'd thought.

She'd walked to the side of the van and seen that its door was open.

And then…

What happened then?

All she could remember was being struck in the head by something very hard.

And now she was here, bound hand and foot.

With every passing moment, her dazed confusion was turning into fear.

"Where am I?" she said hoarsely.

No one answered.

"Where am I?" she repeated more loudly.

Again there was no answer.

Am I all alone? she wondered.

Had she been bound and abandoned in this dark place, never to be found or rescued?

As adrenaline surged through her body, she let out a scream of rage and terror.

"Answer me! Where am I? What do you want with me?"

When no reply came again, she continued to scream wildly and wordlessly. When she finished, her very panting sounded deafening.

Then a possibility occurred to her.

It's a test of some sort.

A test of faith.

If so, she mustn't scream, mustn't lose heart. She began to murmur aloud.

"Hail Mary, full of grace, the Lord is with thee."

She wished she could reach her rosary, which she could feel hanging around her neck.

Even so, she continued, "Blessed art thou amongst women, and blessed is the fruit of thy womb, Jesus."

Before she could say the next words, she heard a quiet, gentle, male voice.

"Don't worry. I'm here to save you."

She almost fainted from relief at what seemed like a miracle.

My prayer was answered!

The seemingly disembodied voice continued.

"But first . . . I have to know for certain . . . that you'll keep your promise."

"Promise?" she echoed.

"You know what promise I mean. And I know you're planning to break it. You mustn't break it."

She lay there trying to grasp what he might mean. She also realized that she recognized that voice from somewhere. Where had she heard it before? Was it someone she knew?

The man said, "Tell me about it, Sandra. Why do you want to do it?"

Do what? she wondered.

Then it began to dawn on her . . .

Oh, my God.

My promise.

My vow.

"It was a mistake," she said desperately. "I was wrong. I've changed my mind. I'll keep my promise."

She heard the man sigh in the dark.

"Now, Sandra, you mustn't lie to me. I know when you're lying."

Sandra could barely breathe. For some reason she believed him, felt sure that he could tell that she was uttering the slightest falsehood.

But how could she be truthful? Right now, she felt willing to do or say anything, true or not, to get free, to put a stop to whatever was going on right now.

"Talk to me, Sandra," the man said with a voice full of concern. "Tell me why. Tell me so I can help you."

At last she recognized that voice. She knew who it was. The man had seemed kindly enough at the time, but somehow she'd felt afraid of him even then.

And now she knew she'd been right to feel afraid.

In a trembling voice, she continued ...
"Holy Mary, Mother of God, pray for us sinners ..."
She choked on the last words, and for a moment couldn't say them aloud.
But I've got to say them.
She forced the words through her lips
"...now, and at the hour of our death. Amen."
She knew in her heart that the hour of her death had arrived.

CHAPTER TWELVE

Riley was already out of bed and getting herself ready to meet Agent Crivaro for breakfast when she heard a sharp knock on her motel room door.

When she opened the door, Crivaro was standing there looking worried and agitated.

"We're needed, Riley," he said. "Right away. Let's grab something to eat while we're driving."

As they walked toward the motel lobby, Riley asked him, "Has there been another murder?"

"I don't know," Crivaro said. "That's what we've got to find out."

At the motel's breakfast buffet, they snatched up rolls and cups of coffee, then headed out to the vehicle the local police had lent them yesterday. Before he started the engine, Crivaro handed Riley a map.

"I need you to give directions," he said to her. "We're headed for Boneau, across the border in Kentucky."

Riley found the location, just a short drive to the northwest. Soon they were on their way, munching their rolls and sipping their coffee as Crivaro drove past farmlands and woodlands on their way to the new town. The roads were completely clear of snow and there wasn't much traffic along the way.

Crivaro finally explained what was going on.

"I got a call from Sheriff Quayle just now. A girl seems to have gone missing at Magdalene Catholic High School in Boneau. Her absence was noticed just this morning, so normally it would be too early for a missing person report. But as you know, Quayle put out an APB to all the towns in the area yesterday, and he told citizens to report any disappearances right away. So the school principal called about it this morning, and then Quayle called me."

Riley asked, "Did Quayle tell you anything else?"

"Only what I just told you," Crivaro said. "I don't think he knows anything else himself."

"Maybe it's nothing," Riley said. "I mean, kids *are* kids. Maybe this one just wanted to be on her own for a while."

Crivaro growled under his breath.

"Maybe, but I don't like the sound of it," he said. "A missing student seems awfully close to what little we know about the killer's MO. If there's been another abduction, the good news *might* be that the victim probably isn't dead yet. Both of the other victims seem to have been held for a while before they were killed. But if that's what's going on, we've got no time to lose."

They drove on for a few minutes without saying anything. Riley sensed a lot of tension in Crivaro's silence.

Is he still mad at me about yesterday? she wondered.

No, this seemed different to her somehow.

She said cautiously, "Um . . . is there anything we need to talk about?"

"No," Crivaro said gruffly. "Why do you ask?"

"I don't know," Riley said.

"Well . . . nothing's wrong, except the usual murder and mayhem in our lives."

Something in Crivaro's tone told Riley otherwise.

She sat gazing at him silently.

"What are you looking at?" Crivaro asked.

"Something seems wrong," Riley said with a shrug.

Crivaro said sharply, "Look, Magdalene High is a Catholic school. I've kind of got a thing about Catholic schools. Okay?"

He said it with a note of finality, as if that explained everything. Of course it didn't.

Riley kept right on looking at him and waited for him to continue.

Finally, Crivaro shook his head and sighed.

"I was raised in a strict Catholic family," he said. "I went to our parish's parochial school when I was a kid."

"I guess you didn't like it very much," Riley said.

Crivaro scoffed. "Yeah, you might put it that way. I guess you've heard all the horror stories about Catholic schools. Super-strict discipline, loads of guilt and shame over every little thing. A lot of that stuff was true, at least in the school where I went. But the worst thing . . ."

Crivaro's squinted and frowned.

Riley was beginning to feel concerned now, but she didn't say so. She figured Crivaro would tell her if he really wanted to. She turned her attention back to the map and the road ahead.

Finally Crivaro said, "When I was little, I had a little dog named Scruffy. A fox terrier, cute little guy. He was … well, I guess you could say he was my best pal. He was always there for me, even when nobody else was. And believe me, there were times when I really needed a friend in those days."

Riley heard Crivaro's voice tighten with emotion. It occurred to her that he'd never talked to her about his childhood before. It was hard to imagine this tough and successful FBI agent as a vulnerable child. It didn't sound as though that part of his life had been very happy.

Crivaro continued, "One day Scruffy got hit by a car and died."

Riley gasped.

"I'm sorry," she said.

"Yeah, it was tough, but I believed everything they told us in church and taught us in school. So when the nun who taught our class asked me how I felt about losing my dog, I told her I was sad, but not too sad. After all, I knew I'd see Scruffy again in heaven someday when I died too. And then we'd be together forever."

Crivaro's face tightened.

Then he said, "Well, the good sister told me that was never going to happen. Scruffy was just an animal, she said, and animals don't have souls, and so they don't go anywhere when they die—not hell, not purgatory, and certainly not heaven. I was never going to see him again, she said."

Riley was shaken to hear the tremor in Crivaro's voice.

"That was a terrible thing to tell a kid," she said.

"Yeah, it was, wasn't it?" Crivaro said. "And the worst thing was, how *cold* she sounded about it. Adults can be real assholes sometimes."

Crivaro fell silent for a moment.

Then he said, "Well, when I finally left that school, I swore never to set foot in a Catholic school again for the rest of my life. I've kept that promise until now."

Riley stammered, "I'm so sorry, Agent Crivaro. Maybe you shouldn't—"

Crivaro interrupted in a surprisingly sharp tone.

"Shouldn't what? Do my job?"

"Well, maybe I could talk to the principal alone, or Sheriff Quayle could go with me instead, or—"

"Don't be ridiculous. I'm not a kid anymore. I'll be fine."

He growled slightly as he stared at the road ahead.

"I might not be at my best, that's all. I need for you to be especially sharp."

"Don't worry," Riley said.

Crivaro drove on in silence for a minute or two.

Then he said, "I've never told anybody about that before. And I'd appreciate it if...well, we could just keep it between the two of us."

"I will," Riley said.

She was touched that Crivaro had confided in her like this. But she also sensed that he might feel defensive about letting his emotional guard down. She knew that he liked to keep his feelings to himself.

Riley turned her attention back to the map, hoping this conversation wouldn't become an issue between them. It was only about a half-hour drive from Dalhart to the little town of Boneau, Kentucky. They traveled the rest of the way in silence except for her occasional directions.

As they drove into Boneau, it struck Riley as almost identical to Dalhart at first—a sleepy little town that felt cut off from the rest of the world. But Riley and Crivaro were in for a surprise when they approached the Magdalene High School campus.

The school looked majestic, venerable, and prosperous. It was dominated by a picturesque, venerable, castle-like building with conical towers. Other smaller structures were clustered around it amid spacious wooded grounds. Beyond the grounds was a clear view of the massive Mississippi River. Riley had never seen it before, and even at this distance its sheer vastness took her breath away.

The whole place struck Riley as perfectly beautiful, with a thin layer of snow adding sparkle to the scene. She could imagine how lush and colorful the campus must be in the spring or fall.

Crivaro parked, and they got out of the car. As they headed toward the main building, they saw a mix of male and female students walking along the broad paths among the buildings, all of them wearing warm jackets over their school uniforms.

Riley noticed a look of amazement on Crivaro's face as they walked along. She could understand why. Most of the students were smiling, and all of them appeared relaxed, happy, and very much at ease here. She saw no hint of shame or anxiety anywhere she looked. This was surely nothing like the school where Crivaro had endured so much childhood unhappiness.

They went inside the main building and found the administrative office. The receptionist sent them into an office to meet the school's principal, Sister Agnes O'Connor.

Sister Agnes was a smiling, hearty, handsome woman wearing a white habit and a wimple. Riley and Crivaro produced their badges and introduced themselves. She invited them to sit down with her at a broad, antique desk surrounded by bookshelves of burnished wood.

With a look of deep concern in her eyes, she said, "Please don't take this the wrong way, but I hope I'm wasting your time and we've got nothing to worry about here at Magdalene."

"We're hoping so too," Crivaro said. "But I'm sure you did the right thing by reaching out like you did."

"Tell us about your missing student," Riley added.

Sister Agnes's forehead crinkled a little.

"Student?" she said. "Oh, she's not a student. Sister Sandra Hobson is a member of our faculty. She's twenty-six years old."

Riley and Crivaro exchanged looks of surprise. Because the other two girls had been students, they'd both assumed that the person who had gone missing here was a student as well.

This changes things, Riley realized.

But she didn't yet know exactly in what way, or how much.

"Let me explain," Sister Agnes said. "Most of our faculty are laypeople, and not all of our students are Catholic—far from it, really. We've got just a handful of nuns and monks teaching classes. Sister Sandra's status here is rather unique. Let me show you."

Sister Agnes's fingers rattled over her computer keyboard for a moment. Then she turned the screen toward Riley and Crivaro. She'd brought up a page about Sister Sandra that had been posted on the school's website. It included a personal statement from the young woman herself, and of course her picture.

Riley was immediately struck by how different Sandra Hobson looked from the two victims so far. She, too, had an open and innocent expression. But there was no mistaking her for a child. There was an earnest maturity and a feeling of serious purpose in her very smile.

Sister Agnes explained, "Sister Sandra is a novitiate, still three years away from full sisterhood. She became a postulant several years ago at the Sisters of Saint Rose Convent over in Trueblood, a town not far from here."

"A postulant?" Riley asked.

Riley had no real knowledge of Catholic life, and she hadn't had any religious training to speak of.

Crivaro put in, "A postulant is sort of a beginner, a nun at the earliest stage of her training."

"That's right," Sister Agnes said with a nod. "Sandra finished all that, and she came here as a mission novitiate two years ago. Teaching is the service she has chosen in preparation for her first vows, which are coming up next year."

Crivaro asked, "When did you notice she was missing?"

"This morning, when she didn't show up for the morning prayers we hold for the monks and nuns," Sister Agnes said. "She's never done that. Ever. And then we couldn't locate her anywhere on campus. I would have worried in any case, but yesterday we'd heard over the radio about those two poor murdered girls, and the warning to stay indoors at night. The bulletin also said to immediately report anyone who might be missing. So that's what I did."

In a cautious voice, Crivaro said, "Sister Agnes, do you have any reason to think she might have . . ."

"Run off?" Sister Agnes said, finishing his thought.

Crivaro nodded and said, "Maybe she finally realized that she wasn't cut out for a life as a nun."

Sister Agnes chuckled slightly.

"I find that very hard to imagine, Agent Crivaro," she said.

"But not impossible?" Crivaro asked.

Sister Agnes sat quietly without answering.

"Just how well do you know her, Sister Agnes?" Crivaro asked.

"About as well as anybody else, I think," Sister Agnes said. "I'm her mentor. There's not much she doesn't tell me. We're exceptionally close. I'm pretty sure she even tells me whatever she winds up telling the priest in confession."

"Yeah, but there's a difference between what she tells you and what she confesses to a priest," Crivaro said. "There's no real 'Seal of Confession' keeping you from telling us whatever she has told you."

Sister Agnes sighed and said, "Oh, I beg to differ, Agent Crivaro. The church doesn't have to put its seal on every little thing to give it sanctity. I take Sister Sandra's confidence very much to heart."

"Surely you can tell us a few things," Crivaro said.

Sister Agnes looked at Crivaro intently.

"She's restless, Agent Crivaro," she said. "I think I can tell you that much, because it's not really any secret around here. She's as devoted to her calling as a novitiate can possibly be. But she's getting impatient. Like I said before, she's still three years away from her perpetual vows. She wishes it were tomorrow. Or better yet, today."

She held Crivaro's gaze for a moment, then added, "A lot of novitiates go through this phase. I felt the same way myself when I was at Sandra's stage in my training. But I hardly believe it's any indication of a desire to run away. If anything, I'd say it means that her devotion is intensifying with time."

Crivaro squinted at her without replying. Riley sensed that her partner was drawing a rather different conclusion from what Sister Agnes was telling them.

Something else was bothering Riley. If Sister Sandra really had been abducted, just where and how had it happened?

Riley said, "Sister Agnes, were all of your students and staff aware of the public warning not to go out alone at night?"

The principal nodded.

"I made an announcement over the PA system," she said. "I'm sure everybody knew about it."

Riley said, "Do you think Sister Sandra might have ignored that warning?"

"I wish I could say no," Sister Agnes said. "But she loves her nighttime walks on the school grounds. She sometimes suffers from insomnia, and she finds it helpful to walk. And she might have found it hard to take my warning very much to heart. Magdalene is always such a safe, nurturing place. There's never a hint of danger here."

Sister Agnes shook her head and said, "I do hope nothing awful has happened. But I can't imagine her just disappearing like this."

"What about your students?" Crivaro asked. "Do they know about Sister Sandra's disappearance?"

"I don't think so," Sister Agnes said. "As soon as we noticed she was gone, I had another sister take over her classes, and I instructed her to say that Sister Sandra wasn't feeling well today."

Sister Agnes blushed and added, "A little white lie, you might say. I don't remember the last time I was the least bit untruthful to anyone here at Magdalene. But I didn't want to cause a panic."

"You did the right thing," Riley said. "Could you show us around the grounds a bit?"

"I'd be glad to," Sister Agnes said.

As they left the principal's office and followed the principal out of the building, Crivaro muttered something in Riley's ear.

"Let's keep this short. We're wasting our time here."

Riley was startled and dismayed. She didn't think they were wasting their time here at all.

In fact, she had a very bad feeling about Sister Sandra's disappearance.

CHAPTER THIRTEEN

Riley's apprehension deepened as Sister Agnes took them on a tour of the campus. Magdalene Catholic High School struck her as lovelier by the moment. But Riley knew that that hardly meant that this place was untouched by evil.

It might mean the opposite, Riley thought.

Some monster might take great satisfaction in wreaking terror on such a beautiful, peaceful setting.

The principal led them through the school's various buildings, where they saw classes in session. They also got to see the gymnasium, the library, and the lunch facilities. Riley couldn't remember ever seeing a school quite like this. Something Sister Agnes had told them back in her office echoed in her head.

"Magdalene is always such a safe, nurturing place."

Riley sensed that Jake, too, was impressed by what he saw. But she also noticed that he kept looking at his wristwatch.

He's anxious to leave, she thought.

That struck her as odd. She didn't share his apparent certainty that they were wasting their time here.

Finally Riley asked the principal to take them where she thought that Sister Sandra might have been walking the night before. Sister Agnes led them outside through the school commons, then out into the grounds that surrounded the campus.

The grounds were well-groomed, and the wide walking path led out into spacious woods. Riley tried to imagine how things would look here at night. There were a fair number of lamps that would brighten the scene, adding to its quaintness and charm.

Sister Sandra might have been alone, but she wouldn't have been walking in the dark. If she had been abducted, Riley figured that her attacker must have been very bold and aggressive.

Or maybe somebody she knew, Riley thought.

If so, might it have been somebody the other victims had known as well? And who might that have been in these separate locations? So far, they had no reason to think the victims had known each other. But that didn't mean that the killer hadn't known all of them. After all, the towns weren't all that far apart.

Finally the path opened onto a field at the edge of the Mississippi River. Riley felt awestruck at the majestic sight and all the history it represented. She wondered—how had settlers felt centuries ago when they reached these banks and faced this staggering expanse of water, at once so peaceful and so powerful?

For a moment, Riley felt too staggered to contemplate the awful thing that might have happened here. It was only during their walk back toward the main building that the ugly possibility began to sink in again.

She looked all around, hoping to glimpse some trace of where an abduction might have taken place. She saw nothing suspicious anywhere. But then, she didn't really know what she ought to be looking for.

She thought back to the crime scene that she and Crivaro had visited when they first arrived in Tennessee—the spot where Kimberly Dent's body had been found. She remembered getting just a fleeting sense of the killer's mind there.

She hadn't sensed any anger or hostility or even shame about him. The crime scene had been much too orderly to suggest such turbulent emotions. Instead, she'd sensed that he'd taken a sort of satisfaction in his deed, almost as if he'd done his duty in taking an innocent girl's life.

Then something dawned on Riley about the killer.

He'd feel comfortable here.

This tranquil, lovely place would probably be just to his liking.

And abducting a young woman on one of these walking paths would suit him perfectly.

I've got to talk to Crivaro about this, she thought.

She needed to persuade him that they should spend more time here.

But as they arrived back at the main building, Crivaro obviously had different ideas.

He said to the principal, "We appreciate your time, Sister Agnes. Once again, you were right to get in touch with us about this. We'll let you know immediately if we have any news."

Sister Agnes thanked him, but there was a note of anxiety still in her voice. Riley could imagine what the principal must be thinking. She was wishing that Riley and Crivaro could offer her some assurance that her novitiate was safe and sound somewhere, and she had nothing to worry about.

Of course, they could assure her of no such thing.

Meanwhile, Riley felt a bit dazed at the rush Crivaro seemed to be in to get away from here. She had to quicken her pace to keep up with him as they headed back toward the parked car.

"Where are we going?" she asked.

"We're going where we've got some *real* business," Crivaro said brusquely. "We're driving to Brattledale to see what we can find out about the first victim."

"But what about Sister Sandra?" Riley said.

Crivaro scoffed, "She'll turn up on her own, I'm sure."

"You mean you don't think—?"

"That she was abducted? No, I don't."

"Why not?"

"Because it would be inconsistent with the killer's behavior. The minute I heard she wasn't a student, and certainly not a teenager, I knew this was a blind alley. Our killer's got a taste for young girls. We can't be sure of much, but we can be pretty sure of that."

"But what about Sister Sandra's behavior?" Riley said. "Sister Agnes doesn't believe she'd run away like that. In fact, she said that she thought Sister Sandra's devotion was growing with time."

Crivaro grunted and said, "If you ask me, Sister Agnes isn't much of a psychologist. She wants to believe what she wants to believe about her protégé. But she said it herself—the girl was 'restless.' That's the key word as far as I'm concerned. It means she wanted out of the cloistered life, but didn't want to tell her mentor about it. So she just took off last night. Sister Agnes probably knows that deep down, but just won't admit it."

Riley stammered, "But—but her disappearance—wouldn't it be a real coincidence if—?"

Crivaro interrupted again, "If what? She happened to disappear around the time the other girls were murdered? Riley we've talked about this before, and you've really got to get it through your head. Coincidences are a fact of life in our business. They're even inevitable from time to time. You take them for what they are, and then you move on. Otherwise you get tripped up by confirmation bias. If you're not careful, everything you see looks like evidence for what you want to believe."

"But I don't *want* to believe anything," Riley said.

"That's good," Crivaro said. "Try to keep on that way. Believing screws up your judgment."

Then under his breath, he said, "Me—I stopped believing a long time ago."

Riley was startled to realize he wasn't talking about the case when he said that. He was talking about his own upbringing, which had soured him on religion. He just couldn't put himself in the shoes of someone who might joyfully pursue the kind of life Sister Sandra wanted for herself—the kind of life that Sister Agnes had embraced for many years.

So which one of us has a real problem with confirmation bias? she wondered.

Riley tried to talk herself out of pursuing the subject. But she couldn't shake the feeling that she was right that Sister Sandra had been abducted and was surely in great danger right now—if she wasn't dead already. Riley just couldn't ignore her own instincts. She had to come right out and speak her mind.

She looked long and hard at Crivaro, then said, "That place really pushed your buttons, didn't it?"

"What do you mean?" Crivaro said.

"I mean Magdalene High School," Riley said. "You went there expecting some kind of emotional hellhole, like the school you went to as a kid. But it wasn't like that at all. It was really lovely, and everyone there was happy. And that really bugged you, didn't it?"

"You don't know what you're talking about," Crivaro said.

"Yeah, I think I do," Riley said. "You could have coped with it if it was as bad as you'd expected. If it had been, we might even still be there right now trying to find out what happened to Sister Sandra. But what you saw there really messed with your head. You found yourself wondering what your whole life would have been like if—"

"If what?" Crivaro snapped. "If I'd gone to a school like Magdalene instead of where I did go to school? Okay, then, I can admit that. The thought did cross my mind. And that place did push my buttons. It bothered the hell out of me. But you know what? It doesn't matter. Because I don't let my emotions interfere with my judgment."

Then in a near-whisper, he added, "Unlike someone else I know."

Riley's mouth dropped open.

"What do you mean by that?" she said.

"Nothing," Crivaro said with a wave of his hand. "Nothing at all."

"No, I want to know what you meant."

"And I don't want to talk about it," Crivaro said. "Suffice it to say you're way out of line. I just want you to respect my years of professional experience. And right now, everything I've learned over the years tells me that whoever killed those two girls wouldn't have been the least bit interested in Sister Sandra. And if we get hung up looking for a woman who might not even want to be found right now, we'll be wasting precious time. Somebody else could die."

Riley said nothing. She was still stinging from his suggestion that she was somehow failing to be objective. But she sure didn't want to pursue the subject.

Meanwhile, Crivaro had been following highway signs to Brattledale.

Crivaro said, "Since we've got that settled, I need for you to do two things for me. I need for you to get on your cellphone and call the county sheriff over in Brattledale and tell him we're on our way, and that we want to talk to Natalie Booker's parents. Then I need for you to get out that map and make sure we don't get lost on the way there."

Still seething inside, Riley took out her cellphone and started to do exactly as she was told. But as she punched in the number for the Brattledale police department, she couldn't help but glance back toward the school they were leaving behind.

Something bad happened there, she thought.

I can feel it.

CHAPTER FOURTEEN

Riley was worried about the bottled-up anger in the car. She and Crivaro managed to drive the rest of the way to Brattledale without getting into another fight. But Riley didn't like how things felt between them, and she was sure Crivaro felt the same way. Sooner or later they were going to have to get their feelings out. She didn't look forward to whatever it was going to take to resolve things between them.

It's not going to be pretty, she thought.

As they pulled into Brattledale, it almost eerily reminded Riley of Slippery Rock, the little town where she had spent part of her childhood. Unlike that Virginia town, Brattledale wasn't nestled in a mountainous valley. But as they drove down the main street, Riley could almost believe that downtown Slippery Rock had been transplanted into this flatter countryside.

There were all the same businesses and buildings—a drugstore, a movie theater, a church, a diner, a bank, a volunteer fire department—many of them with the same architectural false fronts she remembered from Slippery Rock. Like Dalhart, Brattledale was a county seat with its own courthouse, but it was a much smaller courthouse and a much smaller town.

They parked in front of the county police station. As Riley and Crivaro got out of the car, a pudgy man in a sheriff's uniform came walking out of the station toward them, smiling widely and shaking hands with them.

"You must be our fed friends," he said. "If you don't mind my saying so, it's about time you showed up. I'm Jim Cole, the county sheriff, and I've got to admit that me and my boys are way out of our league dealing with this murder business. I sure hope you can give us a hand."

Riley was startled by how different this greeting was from when Sheriff Quayle had met them at the airport yesterday.

I guess some locals don't hate the FBI after all, she thought.

Sheriff Cole said, "I understand you want to talk to poor Natalie's mother. Let's drive over and see if we can catch her at home. I'll tell you how to get there."

As the three of them got into the car, Riley asked Cole, "Shouldn't we call ahead and see if she's available?"

"Hannah Booker doesn't have a phone," Sheriff Cole. "She doesn't have much of anything electrical—no computer, not even a TV, I don't believe. But there's a good chance we'll find her this time of day."

Cole rattled off some directions, and as Crivaro started to drive, he filled the sheriff in on what he and Riley had been doing since they'd started working on the case yesterday.

"Doesn't sound like you're making much progress," Cole said. "And I'm afraid talking to Hannah won't do you much good. I spent a good long time talking to her, and I don't think she knows anything. She's kind of a basket case, if you want to know the truth."

Riley said, "I can't imagine how hard this must be for her."

"Oh, it's hard, all right," Cole said. "But she's been pretty much a basket case for years, ever since she and I were in high school together. She got pregnant with Natalie when she was sixteen, poor kid. Everybody knew who the father was—an older boy named Elmer Clay."

Cole shook his head and continued, "Hannah never said so, though. And Elmer never admitted the kid was his. A real jerk, that guy. Everybody in town always knew he wouldn't amount to anything, and we were more right than we knew. He got drunk and killed himself by driving into a tree a couple of years after Natalie was born."

Riley's curiosity was piqued.

"So what happened to Hannah?" she asked.

"Well, she managed to raise Natalie on her own," Cole said. "She's been working at whatever kinds of jobs she can get all these years—cleaning houses, dishwashing at the local diner, doing laundry, menial stuff like that. She was never especially bright or capable, so she depends a lot on people's kindness and charity. Fortunately, there's still some of that kindness and charity in these parts."

Cole sighed and added, "The truth is, Hannah has regressed emotionally. During the last three or four years, Natalie got to be more of a mother to her than Hannah ever was to Natalie."

Crivaro asked, "What about Natalie? Did you know anyone who might have meant her any harm?"

"Oh, no, everybody loved her," Cole said. "She was a good kid, a bright kid, kind and super responsible and mature. You'd never have believed she'd grown up in those kinds of circumstances."

"Did she have a boyfriend?" Crivaro asked.

"Yeah, I guess you could say that," Cole said. "She'd been dating Dick Haley, another older kid, but a really good guy, a star athlete and a great student and an Eagle Scout. He joined the army a year ago, and he's stationed at Fort Hood in Texas. He stopped in town on leave about a week and half ago, shortly before Natalie was killed, and they spent some time together."

"Do you think . . . ?" Riley began.

"Not a chance," Cole said. "Not that I'd ever suspect Dick of anything like that, I still went to the trouble of eliminating him. I confirmed with the staff down at Fort Hood that he was back there at the time of the murder. I interviewed him over the phone, and he couldn't imagine who would have done such a thing. Poor guy was awfully shook up about it. He couldn't get another leave to come back for Natalie's funeral."

Riley got the feeling that Cole was one small-town sheriff who was really good at his job. She doubted that he'd left a single stone unturned. And if Hannah Booker knew anything at all about her daughter's death, Cole would have already found out about it.

This is probably going to be a wasted visit, she thought.

She wished more than ever that Crivaro hadn't dragged them away from Magdalene High School. She couldn't help thinking they still had some unfinished business there.

Cole directed Crivaro to stop in front of a shabby, one-story wood-frame house in an otherwise pleasant neighborhood. The three of them got out of the car and walked up to the door and knocked.

The woman who answered the door looked tired and worn and extremely thin.

Cole took off his hat respectfully and said, "Hannah, I hate to trouble you any more, but these two are from the FBI's BAU—Agents Crivaro and Sweeney."

There was just a flicker of life in the woman's dull eyes.

"Oh—have you found anything about what happened to Natalie?" she said.

"I'm afraid not," Cole said. "But they'd like to talk to you."

That flicker vanished, and her eyes went dead again.

"I can't imagine why," she said. "And I'm awfully tired of talking about it."

Hannah Booker was standing square inside the front door, not offering any invitation for her three visitors to come inside. Crivaro didn't seem to want to press the issue. As they stood on the porch in the cold air, Riley listened as Crivaro asked Hannah a few questions and she answered as well as she could.

She's said all this before, Riley guessed.

As the questions and answers continued, Riley noticed something odd about Hannah's voice and manner of speaking. She spoke very quietly, but in a high-pitched, babyish voice, and an almost eerily singsong manner.

Like a child, Riley thought, remembering Cole's remark that Hannah had regressed emotionally over the years.

Riley wondered—had this woman ever really grown up? Living life as a single mother in a small town like this must have taken a terrible toll on her. Her youth had been taken from her at the age of sixteen. Perhaps her ability to grow up emotionally had been taken from her as well.

Riley remembered something that Cole had said.

"Natalie got to be more of a mother to her than Hannah ever was to Natalie."

Everybody in town seemed to think very highly of Natalie, especially her mature and responsible nature. Had Natalie been forced to grow up fast because her mother had never grown up at all? All Riley knew for sure was that this woman was going to have a very hard time in life without her daughter's steadying hand.

It's so sad, Riley thought.

Hannah finally interrupted Crivaro's questions.

"It's kind of you to try to find whoever did this. But you can't. You'll never succeed."

"Why not?" Crivaro asked with surprise.

Hannah heaved a long sigh and said, "Because it's not God's will. If God had wanted her killer to be found, he'd have let it happen by now. But he didn't."

With a determined expression, Hannah nodded and said, "And that's all right. I understand everything now. God took Natalie away while she was still good, and she's in heaven now. He wasn't punishing her. He was punishing me. And I deserve it because of how I sinned all those years ago."

Sheriff Cole looked distressed by what he was hearing.

He said, "Now Hannah, don't talk that way."

Hannah smiled strangely and said, "Thanks so much for dropping by. I hope you'll stop troubling yourselves about all this. Things are as they should be, and there's nothing more to be done about it."

Without another word, she stepped back and shut the door, leaving Riley and her two colleagues standing on the porch.

Sheriff Cole raised his hand to knock the door, but Crivaro stopped him.

"Don't bother, Sheriff. She's got nothing more to tell us."

The sheriff just glanced at Crivaro and nodded, and they returned to the car.

As they drove to the police station, Riley remembered Hannah's words.

"God took Natalie away while she was still good . . ."

An idea was taking shape in Riley's mind about these sad young victims. But she couldn't yet put her finger on exactly what it was or what it could mean.

CHAPTER FIFTEEN

All during the drive back to Dalhart, Riley couldn't get Hannah Booker's words out of her mind. The woman considered herself a sinner, but was sure that her daughter Natalie had been utterly good.

"She's in heaven now," the woman had said with absolute conviction.

Of course that belief was to be expected in a woman of such faith, but Riley could feel something about those words nudging her toward a broader idea. She couldn't quite get hold of it.

She glanced at Agent Crivaro. He had a frown on his face as he concentrated on his driving. She wished she could talk it over with him, but he had barely said a word to her during the whole drive. In fact, he had been out of sorts with her ever since their earlier disagreement.

Actually, Riley felt pretty sure that another argument was all but inevitable. But she wanted to put it off for as long as she could—maybe until something positive happened with the case that made their differences seem less significant.

Their visit to Brattledale had been surprisingly short. After their brief conversation with Hannah Booker, Crivaro and Riley had driven Sheriff Cole back to his police station. On the way there, Crivaro had asked Cole what he had done by way of investigating Natalie's death.

From what he'd said, it was obvious that Cole had done a fine job, especially in his interviews. It sounded as though he'd talked to almost everybody in the small town and asked all the right questions. There didn't seem to be any loose ends for the agents to tie up in Brattledale.

With nothing left to do there, Crivaro had decided that he and Riley should head back to Dalhart to reorient themselves and look for some new strategy to deal with this increasingly frustrating case. But Riley wasn't sure how they were going to exchange productive ideas, so she just leaned back in the car seat and kept quiet for the rest of the short drive.

When they got back to the police station in Dalhart, they met with Sheriff Quayle in a small conference room. As Crivaro filled Quayle in on their visit to Magdalene High School, he said something that startled Riley.

"We don't think the nun's disappearance is at all related to the two murders."

Riley could barely keep her mouth from dropping open.

"We?" she thought.

It felt like a slap in the face. Why couldn't Crivaro at least acknowledge that his partner didn't share this belief?

Again, Riley managed to keep quiet to avoid starting an argument right then. But Crivaro kept right on assuring Quayle that the young woman had simply wanted to get away from cloistered life, and that she'd turn up on her own somewhere sooner or later.

If Crivaro noticed Riley's dismay, he didn't show it. He just changed the subject to their visit to Brattledale and what little they'd been able to find out there.

"So what do we do now?" Quayle asked after Crivaro finished briefing him on the day's activities so far.

"Keep looking for a connection between the two murders we know about," Crivaro said. "And look for any related cases."

Quayle shrugged and said irritably, "We've done a lot of homework, and as far as I know, there aren't any related cases."

Crivaro replied calmly, "I know, but let's take a fresh start digging through records."

Together Crivaro and Quayle did a computer search of all the recent homicides in the relevant area of Tennessee and Kentucky. Riley could do little but sit and listen and watch. She couldn't help feeling that Crivaro was deliberately excluding her.

Predictably, Crivaro and Quayle found that most of the homicides were concentrated in larger cities, and there were only a handful in small towns and rural areas. None of them bore any resemblance to the murders of Natalie Booker or Kimberly Dent.

For good measure, Crivaro asked Quayle to show him records of older homicide cases dating back some ten years. Quayle fetched a folder full of reports, and he and Crivaro went through them carefully. A few homicides showed up in that area. A few of those were by what was termed "asphyxiation by ligature"— or strangulation.

"These stats aren't surprising," Crivaro explained to Quayle. "Strangulation is the fourth most common method of homicide, after beating, stabbing, and shooting. Shooting, of course, tops the list."

"But these old strangulation cases were all solved," Quayle said. "Every one of them. The killers were sent to prison. I don't see how there could be any connection between any of them and our recent murders."

"I don't either," Crivaro said. "But there's a possibility we've got to consider. It's not likely, but we can't ignore it."

"And what's that?" Quayle said.

Crivaro drummed his fingers on the table for a moment.

Then he said, "Because strangulation is so common, it's just possible that the two girls were murdered by different people."

Quayle's eyes widened with alarm.

"How could that be?" he asked. "The MO is the same in both cases— abduction followed by strangulation. Also, look at how the bodies were left out in the open. They were even laid out in an identical manner. Are you suggesting some kind of team or partnership or . . . ?"

"What I'm talking about is more like a copycat," Crivaro said. "Details about murders leak out. It happens all the time. Someone here in Dalhart might have learned most of the details of Natalie Booker's killing in Brattledale— someone who had a personal grudge against Kimberly Dent and wanted her dead. He might have used the other killer's MO to cover his tracks."

Crivaro went on to cite some actual cases of this sort, including a couple of cases he'd actually worked on. Riley felt sure that even Crivaro didn't think this was really a likely scenario. But she also knew he was right to consider it, especially since if there were two separate cases this wouldn't be a matter for the FBI, much less for BAU.

Meanwhile, neither man was asking her opinion. Feeling excluded, Riley turned her thoughts back to her own observations about the interviews.

Hannah Booker had said to them about her murdered daughter,

"God took her away while she was still good."

And, *"She's in heaven now."*

Riley felt a tingle of mounting intuition as other memories came back to her.

She remembered Sister Agnes stating her opinion that Sister Sandra's faith was *"increasing with time."*

She also remembered the solemn sight of Kimberly Dent's parents standing with bowed heads in front of the cross-shaped shrine that bore their daughter's name.

And now something else Hannah said echoed through Riley's mind.

"Natalie always went to church and did what was right."

Suddenly, something seemed clear to her.

Crivaro and Quayle were still in mid-conversation, but Riley interrupted anyway.

"Sheriff Quayle, did Kimberly go to church?"

Sheriff Quayle looked startled, but Riley felt as though she already knew the answer.

"Well, yeah," Quayle said. "The Dent family goes to the same Methodist church that I attend with my own family, right here in Dalhart."

Riley looked back and forth at Crivaro and Quayle. Both men were staring at her, but she thought Crivaro looked impatient.

She hesitated for a moment, then she blurted, "It's about religion."

Quayle squinted and asked, *"What's* about religion?"

"The murders," Riley said. "Religion is the thing that links them all together."

Ignored a silent frown of warning from Crivaro, Riley continued, "Hannah Booker told us that her daughter went to church. If she was anything like her mother, she was pretty deeply religious. And then there was Sister Sandra at Magdalene High School…"

It was Quayle's turn to interrupt Riley now.

"Wait just a minute, Agent Sweeney. I thought that her disappearance had nothing to do with the two murder cases."

Riley's spirits sank as she remembered what Crivaro had told him before.

"We don't think the nun's disappearance is at all related to the two murders."

And now she could see Crivaro's face redden with anger.

"My partner misspoke," he said, glaring at Riley.

A tense silence fell over the room, and Crivaro kept his gaze locked with Riley's.

Finally Crivaro said to Quayle, "I think my partner and I need to adjourn for the day. We've got some things we need to talk about one-on-one."

Looking surprised at the suddenness of this decision, Quayle nodded silently. Riley got up and followed Crivaro out of the room and the police station, dreading whatever was about to happen next.

❧   ❧   ❧

Jake was seething as he and Riley walked out to their parked car. He could hardly believe how Riley had blindsided him just now.

Riley said to him, "Agent Crivaro, I'm sorry I brought it up that way, but I really do think—"

"No, you didn't think," Jake interrupted her. "That's the problem."

After they climbed into the car, Jake noticed that it was already getting dark outside. He looked at his watch and said in a tense voice, "It's getting late. We'd better get something to eat. There's a diner right next to our motel."

As he drove to the motel, Jake maintained a grim silence. He was relieved that Riley just sat there without saying another word. There was a lot to say, of course, but Jake didn't want to get started until he felt sure he could keep his temper under control. After he parked the car, he got out and went into the diner without more than a glance at his young partner. She followed him and they sat down and ordered their sandwiches.

As they waited for their meals, Jake leaned across the table and spoke to Riley in a voice that shook with anger.

"Don't you *ever* contradict me again in the presence of local law enforcement. For that matter, don't ever contradict me in front of anybody. I'm your senior partner. Show me some respect."

Her face flushed red with emotion, Riley fingered the rim of her water glass.

"I didn't mean any disrespect—sir," she said.

"Well, it sure as hell sounded like you did," Jake said. "And now Sheriff Quayle knows we're at odds. What do you think that's going to do to his confidence in us? He doesn't think much of us Feds as it is."

"I apologize," Riley said in a tense voice.

Jake didn't reply.

She doesn't sound like she means it, Jake thought.

There was a lot more to be said, but he hardly knew where to begin. He and Riley sat staring at the table until their sandwiches came.

Then Riley spoke up, "I still think we should talk about what I started saying back there."

"I don't want to hear it," Jake said, taking a bite of his sandwich.

Riley's eyes flashed with anger.

"Well, I'm going to tell you, anyway," she said.

Jake's eyes widened with surprise at the sudden sharpness in Riley's voice.

She said, "I think you're wrong about Sister Sandra. I'm pretty sure she's going to be our killer's next victim, if she isn't already. And that's because there *is* a link between her and Natalie and Kimberly. They were all religious. Sandra's preparing to be a nun, and the other girls were serious churchgoers."

"And what does that have to do with anything?" Jake asked.

"It means the killer has some kind of issue with religion," Riley said.

Jake scoffed.

"Come on, Riley. There's a reason they call these parts the Bible belt. Practically everybody around here is religious and goes to church. If our killer is really that obsessed with religion, why doesn't he set off a bomb in one of these towns? Why doesn't he kill as many people as he possibly can? What makes these girls so special?"

Riley didn't reply. She just poked at her sandwich with her fork.

Jake took another bite of his own sandwich, then said, "Your theory doesn't make any sense."

"It's not a theory—yet," Riley said. "It's more like a hunch, and I'm still trying to understand it myself."

"Well, let me know when you do understand it," Jake said. "Meanwhile, don't go making a mess of things when we're trying to work with local law enforcement. Do you hear what I'm saying?"

Again, Riley didn't reply.

As they kept eating in silence, Jake knew perfectly well that nothing was resolved between them—and also that they weren't dealing with Riley's real, underlying problem.

It's time to clear the air, he thought.

He said, "Riley, I've asked you more than once now. Are you sure you're up to working on this case?"

"Of course I am," Riley said.

"I'm not so sure of that," Jake said. "You're obsessing in a non-productive way. And I don't think you even know *why* you're obsessing."

Riley grunted sarcastically.

"Well, I'm sure you're going to tell me," she said.

Jake pushed what remained of his sandwich aside.

He said, "Riley, you're just not dealing with what happened a couple of days ago."

Riley glared at him.

"You mean with killing somebody?" she said.

"That's exactly what I mean. And I'm starting to think that this whole case is a diversion, a way of avoiding the unavoidable. And now you're hatching ridiculous theories to avoid it. You're trying to think about anything else except the fact that you took a human life."

Riley's face twitched with anger.

"You're not a mind reader, Agent Crivaro," she said.

"No, but I'm a pretty damn good profiler," Jake said. "I'm good at reading people—and not just criminals. I know from personal experience what it's like when an agent's judgment is impaired."

Riley pushed her own sandwich aside.

"My judgment's just fine," she said. "And I'm telling you, I'm all but sure that Sister Sandra has been abducted. If she's still alive, the clock is ticking before she winds up dead too—nicely posed by a road, just like Natalie and Kimberly."

Jake and Riley sat glaring at each other for a long moment.

Then Riley said, "We need to go back to Magdalene High School. Right now."

"Why?" Jake said.

"I don't know. I just feel like we missed something when we were there earlier."

Jake reached in his pocket, took out the keys to their borrowed car, and slid them across the table to Riley.

"Go ahead, knock yourself out," he said.

"You're not going with me?" Riley said.

"Nope. You're on your own."

Riley seemed to waver for a moment. Then, without another word, she defiantly picked up the keys and walked out of the diner. Jake sat watching through the window as Riley got into the car and drove away.

He felt momentarily relieved to have her gone.

Now maybe I can hear myself think.

And right now, thinking was exactly what he needed to do. He could walk over to the motel, shut himself up in his room, and collect his thoughts. In the past, some of his best ideas had come to him while sitting alone in a motel room.

And a good night's sleep wouldn't hurt, he thought.

Jake paid the bill for their sandwiches and left the diner. When he felt the cold night air on his face, he was suddenly seized by a spasm of self-doubt.

What if she's right? he thought.

And what if I'm wrong?

He also wondered if maybe he'd come down too hard on Riley about her judgment. He reminded himself that he'd been doubting his own judgment lately. Was it possible that he was just projecting his own insecurities onto her?

Don't overanalyze, he scolded himself as he opened the door to his room and went on inside.

After all, the worst that could happen was that Riley would be right, that she'd come back from Magdalene High School with all kinds of valuable information and insights.

I can live with that, he thought, stretching out on the bed.

Swallowing his pride would be a small price to pay to solve this case.

CHAPTER SIXTEEN

As Riley drove toward Boneau, her mind kept replaying Crivaro's words.

"Go ahead, knock yourself out," he'd growled as he slid the car keys across the table to her.

Obviously, he'd thought she was wasting her time heading back to Magdalene High School, and he didn't want to waste his own time as well. She still felt angry—but more with herself than with Crivaro. Something else he'd said also echoed in her mind.

"I'm starting to think that this whole case is a diversion, a way of avoiding the unavoidable."

Those were the words that had left her feeling defensive. After all, she'd barely given a moment's thought to Heidi Wright's death all day long. But Riley knew perfectly well that didn't mean it wasn't troubling her. Staying busy on the case kept the memory just beneath the surface of her thoughts, delaying what was surely an inevitable moment of reckoning.

She sighed, wondering if maybe she'd needed to hear exactly what Crivaro had said. She knew there was also another issue she was trying to suppress.

Ryan.

She remembered Ryan's words when she'd called him on the phone to say she was taking this case.

"You decided this without even talking to me."

She couldn't blame him for being angry and hurt, especially because she'd spoiled the lovely romantic evening he'd planned for them—an evening she knew perfectly well they both needed.

Worse still, they hadn't spoken since that phone call yesterday morning. And she knew that was more her own fault than his.

I need to call him, she thought.

But what was she supposed to say? That she was sorry she'd rushed off to work on a case? Would that even be an honest thing to say? The truth was, she was doing exactly what she wanted to be doing. And maybe that meant that her work really was more important than her relationship with Ryan.

If so, what kind of person did that make her?

She remembered something else Ryan had said to her the night before last.

"What kind of job is it that makes you feel so terrible about yourself? Is this really what you want to do with your life?"

She had to admit that those were important questions—and also that part of her dreaded finding out the answers. For nearly a year now, since the first murders and investigations when she was still in college, Riley's life had been moving very fast. She had found it easier to put off thinking about some difficult issues, sure that she would catch up later…

The car tires squealed as she rounded a curve.

Too fast!

She forced herself to slow down. It really did feel as though she was trying to drive away from the realities of her life. And her flimsy excuse was that she might find out something by driving to Magdalene High School and doing…

What?

She really didn't know. She thought for a moment about turning around and going back to the motel, telling Crivaro that she really wasn't in any frame of mind to work on this case, and trying to catch the first commercial flight back to DC.

But then she gritted her teeth and reminded herself of her genuine concern about Sister Sandra.

I might be right, she thought.

And Crivaro might be wrong.

If Sister Sandra really had been abducted, time was surely running out for her—if it hadn't run out already. Riley felt like she had to do something. Making this trip to Boneau was surely better than doing nothing at all.

It was dark by the time she parked at the Magdalene High School campus. She got out of the car and shivered sharply from the cold.

What now? she asked herself as she looked around.

She knew that Sister Agnes lived on campus. Although it was dark, it still wasn't very late. Sister Agnes would surely still be awake—if not in her office, then in her living quarters. Riley reached for her phone to call her and ask about meeting with her again right now.

But she hesitated. What questions could she ask the principal that she and Crivaro hadn't already asked during their earlier visit? Riley didn't know. She decided to walk around a bit and try to pull her thoughts together.

As she began wandering along the campus's wide walkways, she reminded herself of something Sister Agnes had told them about Sister Sandra.

"She loves her nighttime walks on the school grounds."

It seemed hardly any wonder to Riley, even on a cold night like this. The lamplight played and sparkled on the snowy ground, and everything was much prettier than it had been during the day.

Trying to retrace Sister Sandra's footsteps, Riley wandered among the buildings and out into the surrounding woods. She tried to guess how Sandra could possibly have been abducted while walking this way, then carried off into the woods.

She found it hard to imagine. The woods were open, not thick, especially now that its leaves were gone. She couldn't see any place where an attacker could have hid in order to take anyone by surprise.

Also, she couldn't imagine how the attacker could have carried a woman off without a struggle, and without leaving some trace of that struggle in the surrounding snow. The walkways had been cleared, but beyond them the snow looked simply pristine everywhere she looked.

She continued out along the path to the edge of the woods and stood looking out over the Mississippi River once again. It was a cloudy night, and she couldn't see very far out over the river, making it seem much larger and more mysterious than it had this afternoon.

An almost eerie feeling of peace began to settle over Riley—the same feeling Sister Sandra must have had during her walks out here. Riley remembered something else the principal had said.

"Magdalene is always such a safe, nurturing place. There's never a hint of danger here."

Riley sighed deeply. She couldn't help feeling that Sister Agnes's words were absolutely true. But if that was so, surely there had been no abduction at all. Agent Crivaro had been right when he'd said that Sister Sandra had left here of her own free will—although right now, Riley found it hard to imagine why anyone would want to leave.

Just as she had this afternoon, she felt nothing but good things about Magdalene High School. And although she couldn't get any sense of the killer's mind here, she could well imagine how Sister Sandra had felt walking here last night—especially if she knew she was about to leave.

She'd have felt sad, Riley thought.

Riley almost hated the idea of leaving here herself.

But it's time to face facts—and life.

She figured maybe it was time to head back to DC after all.

But as she turned to walk away, something unexpected caught her eye.

Something large and white was just a short distance away, on one of the other walkways that meandered through the woods. In the light of the lamps, she could just glimpse it through the trees.

Instead of returning the way she had come, Riley made her way along the other path toward the object. She soon saw that a white van was parked there. Its headlights were on and its motor was running.

Riley felt a jolt of confusion as she wondered—what was a vehicle doing out here on these walking paths?

Surely that's not normal, she thought.

She flashed back to the scene where Kimberly Dent's body had been found, and the indistinct tire tracks that Crivaro had uncovered at the edge of the road shoulder. The tracks had obviously been left by the killer.

"Heavy enough to leave traces," Crivaro had observed, but they hadn't been able to determine what kind of vehicle had left them.

And now she realized it could very well have been a van, a vehicle exactly like this.

More than that, she began to understand how the killer might have made use of such a van—including right here on the school grounds. Surely Sister Sandra wouldn't have expected to see a van here. Perhaps the killer had driven right up to her and caught her unawares and ...

And what?

She wasn't sure. But she did know one thing.

This might be the killer.

But what was he doing back on these paths where he'd abducted Sister Sandra in the first place?

She walked cautiously toward the van. Its driver side was facing her, and it had no side windows except for driver window. It didn't look as though anybody was seated at the wheel.

She gasped as it occurred to her—perhaps he had returned here with the body, and he intended to leave it here, gracefully laid out like the bodies of Kimberly and Natalie. If so, he might be tending to that grim task at this very moment on the far side of the van.

And if so, Riley needed to be ready to confront him.

Her nerves tightened as she drew her weapon and approached the van.

CHAPTER SEVENTEEN

As Riley cautiously moved forward, she noticed that her Glock was trembling in her hands. She knew why. This was the first time she'd drawn her weapon since . . .

Don't think about it, she told herself.

She couldn't let herself get distracted at a time like this. She had to keep herself together.

When she reached the vehicle, Riley hesitated and listened for a moment. She thought she could hear a faint scraping sound from the far side, but she couldn't guess what that might be.

She stepped out from behind the vehicle.

A figure was hunched there on the ground, apparently still unaware of her presence.

She was about to announce that she was FBI and tell whoever it was to put his hands where she could see them. But before she could open her mouth to say anything, the flashback hit her with full force.

Instead of a crouching stranger, she saw Heidi's dead face with its innocent, childlike eyes looking right at her.

She heard a loud clattering sound.

Then a man's voice brought Riley back to the present.

"Holy Mary, Mother of God!"

She saw a muscular, bulky man rising shakily to his feet. Then she realized that she had dropped her gun.

"What do you want?" the man cried as he raised his hands. "Take anything you want."

The sheer terror in his voice told Riley that this was not the killer. If it was, he would surely have grabbed up her fallen weapon, and she might well be dead by now. Instead, she had just crept up on some innocent guy who just naturally assumed he was being robbed.

As she reached down to pick up her gun, she said, "You can relax. My name is Riley Sweeney, and I'm an FBI agent."

She felt herself flush with embarrassment as she said those words.

Some FBI agent, she thought.

She couldn't imagine having handled the situation any more clumsily.

"FBI?" the man said, lowering his hands. He didn't make any comment about the dropped gun. Instead he just asked, "What are you doing here?"

"I'm here on an investigation. I'm sorry I alarmed you."

"Alarmed me?" the man said. "You scared me half to death. What are you investigating, anyway?"

Riley didn't reply. On one hand, she didn't want to tell this man she was investigating two murders and a possible abduction that might have taken place right here. On the other hand, she was still trying to regain her composure. She found herself wondering anew just what anyone was doing with a van out on these walking paths.

"Who are you?" Riley asked.

The man said, "I'm Leroy Stimac, and I'm the groundskeeper here at Magdalene."

He pointed to a trash scoop standing next to a small dead animal lying on the pavement. He began to chatter away nervously

"I was just driving through here making my last rounds for the night when I saw this dead squirrel. I wanted to scoop it up so the students wouldn't see it tomorrow. The kids here are awfully fond of the squirrels around this place, almost like they're pets. They get all emotional whenever anything bad happens to one of them. Hey, you didn't answer my question about what you're here to investigate."

"I'm not at liberty to say," Riley said. It seemed like the best way to avoid telling him the truth.

"Well, okay, then," the man said.

He let out an awkward chuckle and continued his chatter.

"Trouble is, these squirrels are so spoiled and tame, they don't have any survival instincts, and they don't know how to stay out of trouble. What's worse, folks from town drive right along these walking paths, even though we've got signs up saying they're not supposed to. They like to use these paths as a short-cut to the river."

Then he pointed the way Riley had just come and added, "There's a really nice view of Old Man River right over that way."

Of course Riley knew that already.

As Leroy Stimac continued rattling on nervously about squirrels and tres-passing vehicles, Riley's mind began to click away, toying with new ideas. A few moments ago she'd been convinced that Sister Sandra couldn't have been abducted on these paths. But now that she'd been told that vehicles sometimes used these walking paths, she began to see things differently.

The sliding side door of the van was standing open, and Riley could see inside.

Interrupting Stimac's rambling chatter, Riley asked, "Does anybody else use this van except for yourself?"

"Nope. It's just me here taking care of these grounds. Oh, I sometimes hire a hand or two when I need to get something built or repaired. But nobody else drives the van."

Then he resumed talking about squirrels and cars again.

Not really listening, Riley peered into the vehicle. She saw that that it was equipped like a little toolshed, with tools and equipment everywhere. There were no seats inside the sliding door, leaving an empty bed for a workspace. That space was separated from the driver and passenger seats by sturdy wire mesh.

A strange feeling began to creep over Riley.

It took a moment before she realized what it was.

I'm getting a sense of the killer.

The truck's interior brought that feeling into focus. The feeling seemed sharper now than it had yesterday at Kimberly's murder scene.

She could imagine this vehicle emptied of all its tools, its wide metal floor bared and a similar kind of fencing separating the back area from the front seats.

It would be perfect for him, she thought.

And she could picture how it had happened. If he'd known about Sister Sandra's late night wanderings, he could have pulled right up beside her on the path and jumped out of the van and...

No, that wasn't how he did it, she thought.

Sandra could have run away too easily. Riley sensed instead that he had parked here and patiently waited for her to walk into his trap. She wouldn't have felt fearful at the sight of such an innocuous vehicle—not on these peaceful grounds, or even after Sister Agnes's announced warning. The warning might even have slipped her mind completely. The idea that any danger might be lurking out here would have seemed as unimaginable to Sandra as it had to Riley just a few moments ago.

And the killer knew that.

He'd waited patiently for her to walk up to him—either out of simple curiosity at why he was parked here late at night, or to scold him for driving on these grounds when there were signs saying not to. And then...

He pounced.

He'd grabbed her and thrown her into the back of the van, which Riley now imagined having no door handles on the inside. He'd slid the door shut and jumped back into the driver seat and driven away.

But was Sister Sandra conscious?

Or did he knock her unconscious?

She realized it didn't matter one way or the other. The fencing would keep him safe from her, and she couldn't open the door. And he could get away from these grounds without anyone hearing her screams.

Riley shuddered deeply at the vividness of her impressions.

But what was the killer's state of mind when he'd done all this?

She remembered the feelings she'd gotten at Kimberly's murder scene. She'd felt sure that the killer hadn't acted out of anger or hostility. Instead, she'd imagined him feeling a certain satisfaction—even a sense of righteousness.

And now Riley got the same feeling right here.

Although he'd apparently resorted to force to get Sandra into the vehicle, he'd felt no animosity. As far as he was concerned, he'd simply done what needed to be done. Perhaps he'd even imagined he was doing it for her own good.

Force without hostility, Riley thought. *A very unique killer.*

Riley's sense of the killer's mind began to wane, and she became aware again of Leroy Stimac's ongoing chatter as he tossed the dead squirrel into a garbage bag.

"Here's the thing about squirrels that I don't get," he was saying. "We've got thousands of them around here—maybe tens of thousands. And all of them have to die sooner or later, don't they?"

With a shake of his head he continued, "But in all my years working here, I've never run across one that seemed to have died from natural causes. The dead ones are always killed by *something*—usually a vehicle. Where do the rest of them go to die? You'd think there'd be some kind of a vast squirrel graveyard somewhere around here, but there's not. I can't get my head around that."

Riley wasn't in the mood to think about dead squirrels right now.

She asked him, "Did you happen to see anything unusual on these grounds last night? Another vehicle like yours, maybe?"

Leroy shrugged and said, "No, but I left before it got really dark. I'm working unusually late tonight. Why do you ask?"

"Just part of my job," Riley said.

"I wish you'd tell me—"

Riley interrupted, "I'm sorry, but I can't talk about it. Thank you for your time. You've been more than helpful."

As Riley walked back across the campus, she thought again about calling Sister Agnes and asking to meet with her. But it was getting late, and Riley still didn't know what kinds of questions she'd ask the principal. She figured she might as well head right back to Dalhart.

When she pulled into the motel parking lot a little while later, she wondered whether she should wake Crivaro up . . .

To tell him what?

That she had some sort of hunch about how a utility van might have been used to abduct Sister Sandra? She was sure that wouldn't be enough to change Crivaro's mind about anything. So what should she do instead?

Try to get a good night's sleep, she figured.

Not that that's likely.

Her head was crammed with doubts and anxieties. But she did feel sure of one thing.

I'm not ready go back to DC.

I've got urgent work to do right here.

As she parked and got out of the car and went on into her motel room, she thought over what she'd learned back at Magdalene High School.

Or did I learn anything? she wondered.

She couldn't be sure. It was still entirely possible that Crivaro was right, and Sister Sandra hadn't been abducted at all. Riley wasn't a psychic, after all. And her instincts were far from infallible.

But somehow, the sight of the inside of that truck had changed things for her. She now knew that it was at least possible that Sister Sandra had been snatched up on those walking paths.

And if so ...

Riley shuddered with dread.

She's very likely dead by now, she thought.

Chapter Eighteen

As the man drove his van along the dark and empty back road, he thought about the hours he'd spent in the dimly lit room with the young woman who was now in the back of his van. It had seemed like a very long time—much longer than he had spent with the two younger girls.

Almost like a lifetime.

Like the others, she'd been bound hand and foot, and terrified over what was happening to her. He'd asked her the same question he'd asked before.

"Why have you made this choice about your life?"

Like the others, she'd given him no understandable answer.

Although he'd never kept track of the time he spent with each of them, he felt sure he'd put more time and effort into his questioning of Sister Sandra Hobson. That was because he felt more emotionally invested in her than in the others. After all, she was the only one of the three he'd known in the past. Some ten years ago, when she was still a high school student, she had listened carefully to his advice.

Back then, he'd really felt hope for her. She'd seemed to understand the danger she was in, the prospect of terrible suffering if she followed her own notions rather than his counsel. She had promised him to make the right choice, and he'd believed her.

But a few days ago while driving through this area, he'd just happened to run across Sandra again in Boneau. He'd recognized her immediately, although she clearly didn't remember him. He'd said nothing to her at the time, but he'd begun to watch her. It hadn't taken long for him to realize that she was again following those old false ideas about what she wanted to do with her life.

Sister Sandra wasn't going to keep her promise after all. Over the years, she must have forgotten all about his words of wisdom.

He'd decided right then and there that he had to help her. He would try once more to make her see what she was doing wrong. It hadn't been hard to find a moment when he could seize her. Those late night walks of hers offered him the perfect opportunity.

He sighed as he eyed the road ahead, looking for an appropriate place to stop. There had been three of them now, two girls and one young woman, and all of them had made the same promise to him in broad daylight. He'd seized them by night when he'd found out their resolve was weakening, then spent hours and hours with them in the dark room trying to persuade them to renew their promises—but to no avail.

Why do they fail so badly?

The choice he offered them seemed so clear. He was simply giving them the opportunity to escape the torments he himself had suffered.

He shuddered as he remembered all the pain his mother had inflicted on him when he was still a child. He still had the scars from where she'd put out cigarettes on his skin, seared the palms of his hands on the electric stove, and made all those tiny cuts with a utility knife.

And of course, there were torments of the heart.

He still suffered those almost constantly. And those were the worst. Those were the torments he'd hoped to save them from.

When he saw a wide shoulder on the road ahead, he pulled his van over and parked there. Looking around at the trees beside the shoulder, he could see that this was a good place. He got out and walked around to the side and slid the van door open.

A warm feeling came over him as he gazed inside. Sandra was lying on the floor just as he had left her, looking perfectly peaceful.

I've saved her from terrible anguish, he told himself.

I've saved them all.

Each time, he had hoped to accomplish it through other means, but he had succeeded in the end.

"Come on, my dear," he said in a gentle, comforting voice. "Come and rest. Everything's going to be all right after all."

He picked up Sandra's body in his arms and carried her to her resting place.

In death she'll keep her promise, he thought contentedly.

CHAPTER NINETEEN

Something clattered on the ground in front of Riley. She peered through the swirling snow, trying to make out what it was.

Then she heard Crivaro's voice call out sharply.

"Riley! Pick up your weapon, damn it!"

Now she could see that her gun was lying there on the concrete pavement where she had dropped it. She knew she should reach forward and pick it up, but for some reason she couldn't make herself do that.

Suddenly the sound of gunfire broke out all around her, although she couldn't see where any of it was coming from or where it was hitting.

Riley realized that she was back in the motel parking lot back in upstate New York. It was happening again—the gunfight with Heidi Wright and Orin Rhodes.

Now she could see Crivaro crouched down behind a nearby car.

He shouted at her again, "Pick up your gun!"

But when Riley tried to pick it up, she felt weirdly paralyzed, and she just couldn't do it.

What's the matter with me?

Then came a lull in the gunfire and she heard a familiar voice from somewhere behind her.

"Humans aren't like squirrels. Their bodies don't disappear when they die. You find them all over the place."

Riley turned and saw the Magdalene High School groundskeeper, Leroy Stimac. He was pushing a wheelbarrow with young woman's body in it. Blood was gushing from a gunshot wound to her chest.

"Just found this one," the groundskeeper said with a shake of his head. "Poor kid, looks like she was shot. Who would do such a thing to an innocent young girl?"

But the figure in the wheelbarrow wasn't quite dead. Her eyes were wide open, and her mouth worked silently as she gasped her final breaths. Her eyes locked on Riley's with an expression of terrible sadness, and then she fell completely still.

Heidi Wright! *Riley realized with horror.*

Leroy Stimac repeated, "Who would do such a thing to an innocent young girl?"

I did, *Riley almost blurted aloud.* I killed Heidi.

But hadn't that been days ago?

Yes, but I did it again just now. I shot her and then I dropped my gun.

She wondered—was she going to have to kill Heidi again and again for the rest of her life?

Trying not to burst into tears over what she had just done, Riley again tried to bend over to pick up her weapon. But she was stopped by another familiar mocking voice.

"Good luck."

She looked up and saw that it was no longer the groundskeeper pushing the wheelbarrow. Instead it was baby-faced Larry Mullins.

"Good luck," he said again, sneering at Riley smugly.

And she knew where he was going with that wheelbarrow. He was on his way to the courtroom, where he was likely not to be convicted for the murders Riley knew perfectly well he was guilty of.

I should have killed him when I had a chance, Riley thought.

I should have killed Larry Mullins and not Heidi.

Riley knew she couldn't bring Heidi back to life, but here was something she could do.

She reached down again, and this time she was able to pick up the weapon.

She stood upright and pointed the gun and fired.

Then she fired again.

And again.

Riley awoke to realize that the sharp sounds she'd been hearing weren't gunshots at all.

Someone was knocking on her motel room door, and she knew who it must be.

Agent Crivaro.

"I'll be right there," she called out in a voice hoarse from sleep.

But getting out of bed wasn't easy. She'd apparently thrashed around in her nightmares, and she was sweating and so tangled up in the sheets that she could barely more. She managed to pull herself loose, climbed out of bed, and went over to the door.

She opened it and saw Crivaro standing there in the early morning light, holding a food tray.

In a surprisingly apologetic voice, he said, "It's kind of early, but..."

His voice faded and he shuffled his feet.

Then he said, "First, I want to apologize for being an asshole yesterday."

Riley was startled, and she was still too sleepy to know just how to reply. She wondered whether she should apologize in turn. But she wasn't sure what for.

"Uh, okay," she said.

"I brought you a peace offering—coffee and pastries," Crivaro said. "That is, if you don't want to slam the door in my face. I wouldn't blame you if you did."

Riley smiled tiredly and said, "Come on in."

As Crivaro came on into the room, she glanced at the clock. It wasn't extremely early. It was actually just about time for her to get up. Crivaro had obviously been out early. As he began to spread the breakfast snacks on the table, Riley said, "You go ahead and start eating. I'll go get dressed and get more awake."

She took a bundle of fresh clothes to the bathroom and began to get herself ready to face the day. As she did, she remembered the dream she'd just had. She still felt a lingering horror at thinking she'd killed Heidi all over again—and worse, that she might have to do it again and again for the rest of her life.

Thank God it was only a dream.

But then she remembered how Larry Mullins had appeared in her dream, and how easy it had been to pick up her gun and shoot him again and again and again . . .

She shuddered at the memory. It reminded her of something Frankie had said to her the day before yesterday.

"If you'd been able to kill Larry Mullins, maybe you'd find it easy to use deadly force in the future—way too easy."

That was exactly the way it had felt in her dream—much too easy.

Riley paused from brushing her teeth to examine her face in the mirror.

She wondered—was it the face of someone who might someday find killing much too easy, even if it was in the line of duty?

Someday, perhaps soon, she knew she would have to use deadly force again.

What if the person she had to kill wasn't a fresh-faced teenager like Heidi Wright?

What if it was an evil monster like Larry Mullins?

How might that change her as a human being?

Maybe I should talk to Crivaro about it, she thought.

But just yesterday Crivaro had told her, *"I can't be your therapist and your partner at the same time. In fact, I've got no business being your therapist at all."*

She knew that he was surely right. If she could just get through this case without falling apart, a visit to a therapist would definitely be in order. Meanwhile, she had to keep her anxieties to herself and get this job done.

She finished brushing her teeth and got dressed. When she went back into the room, Crivaro was already eating so she sat down at the table with him.

"So what's going on?" she asked.

"Well, you go first," he said. "Did you get any insights at Magdalene High School last night?"

Riley hesitated before replying. But then she told him about her encounter with the groundskeeper, and her sense of connection with the killer while looking into the van. He looked especially interested when she described the van.

Then Crivaro said, "So you really believe Sister Sandra was abducted?"

Riley nodded said, "Actually, I'm afraid the worst has already happened."

"Yeah, well, you might be right," Crivaro said.

Riley was surprised to hear him agree with her.

"I didn't get much sleep last night," Crivaro said. "I kept thinking about what we must be missing. I got afraid I let the fact that Sister Sandra was a teacher and not a student throw me. I realized late last night, I should have listened to you better."

He took another bite of pastry and said, "Anyway, I got up super early and headed for the police station. The folks on the night shift were really surprised to see me there at that hour. And I just started going through random records."

He squinted hard and said, "And I thought, *if* Sister Sandra is one of the victims, they're all linked by one thing—high schools. And I figured that was what I needed to check into."

He sipped his coffee and said, "Well, I went over the work Sheriff Quayle had done here in Dalhart, the interviews and so forth, and he'd been as thorough as hell, just like Sheriff Cole had been in Brattledale. There seemed to be zero chance the killer was a student or teacher or janitor or anything else like that."

Riley felt like she was following his train of thought pretty well.

She said, "You needed to find somebody else—somebody connected to all the schools."

"Right, and I had trouble at first," Crivaro said. "But then I started skimming through local newspapers, and I ran into an article about how old the public buildings are in this whole area—including the school buildings."

Riley nodded. She remembered the picturesque old facade of the main building at Magdalene High School.

Crivaro continued, "And the article said that asbestos is a problem with a lot of those old buildings."

"Asbestos?" Riley asked.

The word rang a bell in her head.

Crivaro said, "Yeah, it used to be used all the time for construction—insulation and ceilings and such. But during the 1970s, asbestos was found to be a dangerous material. It caused cancer. So its use in newer buildings was banned."

Riley said, "But there must have been lots of asbestos left in old buildings."

"Right," Crivaro said. "And getting rid of it can be a problem."

"I can imagine," Riley said. "Getting rid of it means handling it. Who wants to do that when you can get cancer from it?"

Crivaro nodded and said, "Pretty much nobody. Which was why it made the newspapers when a local company was willing to take on the task for this whole area—including the towns of Dalhart, Boneau, and Brattledale."

Riley's eyes widened with interest.

"We've got to find out if that company worked at the three schools."

Crivaro chuckled and said, "No need to check. It said so right there in the newspaper article. The citizens in all three towns were anxious to get their schools cleaned up ahead of anything else. So they found an outfit that would get it done—Mitch's Solutions, about an hour's drive from here."

Riley mulled over what she was hearing.

She said, "So you think an employee with that company...?"

"Is maybe our killer," Crivaro said. "Those jobs would have given somebody an opportunity to get to know Kimberly, Natalie, *and* Sister Sandra, then target them for murder."

Riley couldn't help feeling uncertain. She didn't want to aggravate Crivaro when he was in such an unusually good mood. Still, there were two or three questions she just couldn't overlook.

She said, "Why didn't the local cops notice this connection already?"

Crivaro shrugged, "Well, they're good at their jobs, but they're not FBI agents. And once we showed up, they left most of the thinking to us. The asbestos removal work got done over a long period—a year or more. The local cops wouldn't have known what to look for, especially since they had no reason to give Magdalene High School any thought. I almost missed it myself."

She said, "Even so, somebody would probably have noticed the connection eventually. Wouldn't the killer have been taking an enormous risk?"

Crivaro grunted, "Yeah, but there are two possibilities. One is maybe our killer isn't exactly a mental giant. The other is that he's smart—and extremely arrogant."

"The kind of killer who likes to taunt law enforcement," Riley said.

"Exactly," said Crivaro. "And now you've got this notion that the killer used some kind of utility van. That supports my theory. You can bet they've got one of those at Mitch's Solutions."

Crivaro rapped his knuckles on the table.

"So if we're finished with our snack, let's head right over to Mitch's Solutions and see what we can find out."

As she followed Crivaro out the door to their borrowed car, Riley remembered again her vivid dream—and the sheer delight she had felt when she'd shot Larry Mullins again and again.

It was only a dream, she told herself.

Still, she remembered something else Frankie had said.

"At least we've been able to keep our humanity, our vulnerability, everything that's best about us."

Riley felt a pang of worry.

Just how fragile, how breakable, were her humanity and vulnerability?

Was she somehow eventually doomed to lose what was best about her as a person?

Keep your mind on the case, she told herself.

If Crivaro was right, they might be on the verge of solving it.

CHAPTER TWENTY

During the hour-long drive to Mitch's Solutions, Riley could feel her expectations rising.

Maybe this is it, she thought. *Maybe this will be the break we need.*

Although Crivaro remained silent as he drove, Riley was sure that he was hoping for that too. Based on his recent mood, Riley guessed that Crivaro needed a boost of success right now even more than she did.

Finally a large sign came into view:

MITCH'S SOLUTIONS
HAZARDOUS WASTE REMOVAL SERVICE

Crivaro drove through the opening under the sign and onto the company grounds. There wasn't much to look at. In fact, Riley wondered for a moment whether the place was out of business.

It was mostly a big paved lot surrounded by high chain-link fencing, with a double-wide mobile home planted in the middle. Various building materials were stacked carelessly around the lot, all of them blanketed by a thin layer of recent snowfall. But then something caught Riley's eye.

Several vehicles were parked here and there. Among the cars and tow trucks and pickups, Riley noticed a white, battered-up utility van. It looked much like the one she'd seen at Magdalene High School last night.

She pointed and said, "Agent Crivaro, look."

"I see it," Crivaro said. "This might be it, Riley. Keep your fingers crossed."

They parked right next to the utility van in front of the double-trailer, which they assumed to house the company office. As they walked toward its door, Riley couldn't stop looking at that van.

Are all our answers in there? she wondered.

She wanted to walk right over to it and try the door for a look inside. Instead, she followed Crivaro to the trailer's front door, where a hanging sign announced COME ON IN. OPEN FOR BUSINESS.

When they opened the door to walk inside, Riley was startled by the sight that met her eye. What appeared to be some weird, white, bipedal creature stood facing her from across the room. It looked almost like a polar bear wearing enormous black gloves and some kind of space helmet.

She heard a chuckle from nearby.

A man's voice said, "I see you've noticed Chuckles, our mascot."

Riley turned and saw a well-dressed, gray-haired man standing up at his desk. He was grinning at Riley and Crivaro, obviously relishing their surprise.

Riley turned toward the figure again. Now she could see that it was an empty protective suit of some sort hanging against the wall.

The man came around his desk and said, "When you're in the business of hazardous waste disposal, you've got to be properly and fashionably dressed. We've got a bunch more suits like Chuckles hanging in the closet, ready to go."

Riley glanced around at the rather shabby office area. It was furnished with battered-up desks, chairs, and filing cabinets that she guessed had come from demolition sites. A woman with horn-rimmed glasses was sitting at another desk. Apparently some sort of secretary, she was reading a tabloid newspaper with big sensational headlines and seemed to be barely aware of the visitors' arrival.

The man said, "I'm Mitch Brown, and I own this place. What can I do for you folks?"

Riley and Crivaro produced their badges and introduced themselves.

Mitch's eyes widened.

"FBI," he said. "This sounds serious. What brings you around here?"

Before Crivaro could reply, Mitch said, "Wait a minute. This must have something to do with those two girls getting murdered—the one in Brattledale, the other in Dalhart. An awful business. Folks are starting to think there's a serial killer in these parts. That would make it FBI business, wouldn't it? But what has that have to do with us here?"

Crivaro said, "We'd just like to ask you about some business you've had in this area. We understand you removed asbestos from the high schools in Dalhart and Brattledale, and also the Catholic school in Boneau."

Mitch nodded and said, "That we did. I can't imagine why that's of any interest to you, though. But have a seat, the both of you, and let's talk about it."

Riley and Crivaro sat down in two beat-up stuffed chairs, and Mitch resumed his seat behind the desk. There were several photos on the desk. It looked like Mitch had a large family that included several children and more than a few grandchildren. Riley was a bit surprised to see a picture of a small yacht. She wondered if it actually belonged to the owner of this company.

Mitch said, "You just mentioned Boneau. Did something bad happen at the Catholic school there as well?"

"I'm afraid we can't talk about that," Crivaro said.

"That's understandable," Mitch replied amiably.

Then he turned to his secretary and said, "Opal why don't you bring our guests some coffee?"

Looking markedly more interested in the visitors now that she knew who they were, Opal put down her newspaper and got up to rustle around a counter in the back of the room. She quickly brought cups of stale-smelling coffee to Crivaro and Riley. Riley took a sip, but it tasted too terrible to drink. From the face he made at his first sip, she could tell that Crivaro's coffee was from the same stale pot.

Setting his cup down, Crivaro asked Mitch, "Did you personally supervise any of the work that was done in those places?"

Mitch chuckled again.

"Lord, no," he said. "I haven't done any of the hands-on work for years. I leave it to my boys."

Crivaro asked, "Did the same crew work on the three jobs?"

Mitch scratched his chin and said, "I'm not sure about that. Lately the boys have been taking on different kinds of work, switching teams from time to time."

Opal piped in, "Shawn Lutz is the man you want to talk to."

Mitch nodded and said, "That's right, Shawn's our asbestos specialist. He's due here any minute now, if you don't mind waiting. You'll find him an interesting character, I'm sure. Quite a sense of humor."

Mitch laughed and pointed to the suit and said, "When he puts on one of these outfits, it's like he thinks he's Darth Vader—you know, that character from the *Star Wars* flicks. He breathes hard through the respirator and does the deep voice thing. That's always good for a laugh.

"Sounds like an odd character," Crivaro commented.

"Right," Mitch agreed. "But he's also got kind of a philosophical turn of mind. When he's not working, he's always got his nose in a book of some sort. Persuasive, too, about all sorts of things."

Riley thought she heard a scoffing sound from Opal, but when she glanced that way the secretary had turned her attention to her tabloid again.

Mitch leaned across the desk toward Riley and Crivaro and said, "For example—did you know that God's dead? Not that I've ever been much of a religious man, but talking to Shawn about it convinced me once and for all. Don't guess I'll ever set foot in a church again, no matter how much my wife tries to drag me there."

Riley felt a tingle of interest. She remembered what she had told Crivaro and Quayle yesterday about the murders.

"It's about religion."

Crivaro hadn't believed her then, and judging from his expression, Mitch's words didn't seem to make an impression on him right now. But Riley wondered if maybe her theory was going to prove correct after all. She was very curious to meet this Shawn Lutz character.

Crivaro said to Mitch, "Tell me a little about your business."

Mitch beamed with pride.

"Don't let this ramshackle outfit fool you. We're a prosperous enterprise."

Patting the picture of the yacht, he said, "Hazardous waste has been good to me."

Then he pointed to framed certificates hanging on the walls. "We're fully accredited, too, and my boys really know what they're doing. They're specialists, fully trained and licensed."

"How did you happen to get into this kind of work?" Crivaro asked.

Mitch said, "Years ago I started out in regular construction, but I came to realize there was good money to be made in this kind of business."

He leaned back in his swivel chair and folded his hands together and continued.

"You see, this whole part of the country has fallen into disrepair. Old buildings are full of nasty problems—mold, lead, inadequate wiring, and construction that doesn't meet today's standards."

Crivaro said, "I take it you work as subcontractors."

Mitch nodded and said, "That's right. Renovation and demolition are both thriving businesses in these parts, but the companies that do those kinds of work can't even get started until somebody gets all the hazardous stuff out of their way. That's where we come in."

Swiveling in his chair slightly, he added, "Asbestos is the worst of it. As you probably know, inhaling its dust and fibers can cause lung cancer and meso-thelioma. Of course, nobody knew that until around 1970. It just seemed like handy, cheap, lightweight, flexible material, good for insulation and such. Old buildings everywhere are just full of the stuff."

Then Mitch squinted at Riley and Crivaro.

"But I still don't know what any of this has got to do with a murder inves-tigation. Surely you don't think…"

Mitch was interrupted by the sound of a vehicle pulling up to the front of the trailer.

"That would be Shawn right now," Mitch said, getting up from his chair. "I'm sure he'll be interested to meet you."

The front door opened, and a ruggedly built man in his thirties came inside.

Mitch said to him, "Shawn, these FBI folks say they'd like a word for you."

Riley and Crivaro produced their badges and were about to introduce themselves when Shawn let out a gasp. He whirled around and bolted back out the door.

Riley and Crivaro exchanged glances, then charged out the door after him. Running ahead of her partner, Riley heard a thud and a loud, cursing grunt behind her. She turned to see that Crivaro had stumbled off the stoop at the trailer's entrance and was clutching his ankle.

Riley felt a flash of worry. Crivaro had hurt his ankle during another case about a month ago, and she knew that it still bothered him from time to times.

As she took a step toward Crivaro to offer him some help, he yelled at her, "Don't mind me, damn it! Catch that guy!"

Riley turned and tore after the man, who was already on his way out through the front gate.

He's fast, she realized.

She could only hope that she was faster.

CHAPTER TWENTY ONE

Riley dashed through the gate. She could see Shawn Lutz farther down the road, looking back over his shoulder to see if she was still after him. Then he turned away and kept running. Riley tore after him, but although she was keeping pace with him, she wasn't catching up with him.

After her rigorous physical training at the FBI Academy, Riley was in tip-top physical condition. Of course she knew that this guy did physical labor for a living. He was likely to be as vigorous as she was but she thought that maybe he didn't have her stamina.

If he stays on the road, I might catch up with him.

Almost as if he could read her thoughts, the man suddenly turned, leaped over a ditch, and fled into the surrounding woods.

Damn, Riley thought.

This was going to be harder than she'd hoped.

She wasted no time deciding what to do. Riley leaped the ditch herself and ran at an angle toward him through the woods, hoping to head him off. Fortunately, Lutz couldn't easily disappear among the barren trees. He was still in clear view.

But he was moving fast, and the woods were full of obstacles. Riley found herself running across slippery ground, dodging fallen limbs and tree trunks and icy branches that lashed her face and body. She ignored the pain and hurried on.

Very quickly, she realized that she was gaining on him. Lutz was bulkier than he was, and not as agile, so the rough terrain hadn't given him the advantage after all.

Then, to her surprise, she saw him stop in his tracks.

She slowed down, trotting toward him cautiously. She soon saw the reason for his pause. Lutz was standing on the edge of a steep drop-off. She couldn't tell just how deep the ravine was, but the sight of it had stopped him in his tracks.

As she approached, he turned toward her with an insolent grin on his face.

"So what are you going to do now, FBI lady?" he said. "Arrest me? What if I don't feel like getting arrested?"

Riley was startled by his brazenness. She'd made several arrests during her short time as an FBI agent, but usually with Crivaro's help. And she'd never arrested anybody with an attitude quite like this man's.

When she reached for her Glock, her hand froze.

Draw your weapon, she told herself.

But she just couldn't. She felt like she had in her dream, when she couldn't stoop down and pick up her fallen gun. Worse, Heidi Wright's face flickered yet again in Riley's mind, staring into her eyes as the life fled from her body...

Snap out of it, Riley thought.

"I knew it," Lutz said. "I knew you didn't have the guts..."

With that, he turned away and dropped out of view.

He jumped! she realized.

But as she stepped to the edge of the drop off, she saw that he was actually sliding and scrambling down a steep, rocky slope, deftly managing to stay on his feet.

Riley hesitated, calculating her risks. If she went after him and stumbled, she might get badly hurt. And even if they both managed to avoid falling, he'd reach the bottom first and make a make a mad dash beyond the boulders at the bottom.

There was another option...

It's now or never.

She leaped, free-falling over the steep slope.

Her body crashed into his.

They fell together the rest of the way down, and when they hit the rocks at the bottom his body cushioned hers.

As Riley disentangled herself from Lutz, she realized that he wasn't moving. She struggled to her feet and looked down at him.

He lay completely still.

My God—maybe I've killed him!

To her relief, he let out a loud groan. He was dazed from the fall, but still alive. He barely seemed aware of what she was doing as she straddled his body and handcuffed him behind his back. She hauled him onto his feet and saw that he'd taken a sharp blow to his forehead, but it didn't look very serious.

"Can you hear what I'm saying?" Riley said.

He nodded mutely.

She said, "Good. Because you're under arrest."

Riley looked all around as she read him his rights.

How the hell am I going to get the both of us out of here? she wondered.

But she saw that the slope tapered off, and that the ground was level some twenty or thirty yards away. She prodded him along in that direction, then through the woods all the way back to the road.

As they headed back down the road toward Mitch's Solutions, Riley saw a welcome sight. Their borrowed car was approaching, with Crivaro driving. When he spotted them, he stopped the car and got out.

Limping toward them, he called out, "Don't worry, kid. I'm in hot pursuit."

Riley laughed, glad to see that he hadn't hurt himself very badly.

As Riley and Lutz approached, Crivaro chuckled.

"My, you two look like you've been through the wringer," he said.

"Oh, it was no trouble at all," Riley said, laughing again.

Crivaro patted Riley on the back.

"Nicely done, kid," he said.

Riley felt a pang of guilt at the compliment. What would Crivaro have said if he'd seen her freeze when she'd reached for her weapon?

I can't let that happen again, she thought.

She knew she was going to have to get over killing Heidi Wright.

She just didn't know when or how.

As Jake Crivaro drove their borrowed police vehicle back to Dalhart, he wondered about the suspect who was riding in the back seat. Shawn Lutz was being very quiet.

I guess he takes his right to remain silent seriously, Jake thought.

Riley had securely shackled Lutz to a metal brace back there before she'd gotten into the passenger seat beside Jake. So far their prisoner hadn't said a word during the drive.

Of course, Lutz had looked pretty beat up when Riley brought him in. He might not feel much like talking. Or maybe he was just embarrassed at being captured by a young woman.

Jake smiled as he remembered what Riley had told him about the arrest—how she'd taken a wild leap after Lutz as he was scrambling down a steep slope.

Actually, Riley looked the somewhat worse for the wear herself.

Guess it's lucky both of them survived the fall, Jake thought.

Riley was a tough kid, as Jake knew perfectly well. She was also full of youthful energy, strength and resilience. Jake could remember being like that himself back in his prime. But those years seemed far behind him now. He was finding it hard to remember how it had felt to take off after a suspect like that. Today, he'd fallen down before the chase even got going.

Jake frowned as he remembered his tumble off the stoop back at the trailer.

I really let Riley down.

He glanced over at his partner.

"Hey, Riley," he said in an unsteady voice. "I'm sorry."

"For what?" Riley asked.

Jake grunted and said, "You know."

Riley looked at him for a moment, then it seemed to dawn on her what he meant.

"It's all right," she said. "It worked out okay, didn't it? I'm just hoping you didn't hurt yourself too badly. I know your ankle has been bothering you lately."

"It's getting better," Jake said.

That wasn't completely true, although he didn't think the tumble had made his ankle much worse than it had been already. It had been smashed up a little over a month ago in Utah, when Riley had very effectively stopped an escaping killer by driving their RV into the path of his larger vehicle. His damaged ankle had slowed him down then, and now this was the second time it had kept him from helping her when she'd needed it.

I'm getting old, he reminded himself.

But it wasn't much of an excuse. If he'd just retire, maybe Riley could partner with a younger agent who could keep up with her better. And maybe one who was just as smart as she was.

He grunted under his breath.

There's only one BAU agent as smart as Riley, he reminded himself.

And that's me.

He knew it wasn't mere ego for him to think so. He had a long record of brilliant successes and a reputation for often-uncanny intelligence. But he sensed that his mind was also starting to slow down.

The recent Larry Mullins case had left him feeling especially insecure. He and Riley had caught the baby-faced, child-murdering monster, but they still didn't know what a jury would finally decide—whether they'd find him guilty or not guilty.

Crivaro knew that on that case, Riley had done the best work she'd known how to do.

But surely I could have wrapped that one up better, he thought.

He'd been racking his mind about it, and he couldn't imagine what he should have done differently. But he couldn't help thinking his younger, sharper self wouldn't have left any loose ends to confuse a jury.

He stifled a sigh as he kept on driving. Maybe their current case was going to turn out better, and that the suspect sitting in the back seat would prove guilty beyond any reasonable doubt.

They'd been able to arrest Shawn Lutz for resisting arrest. The fact that he'd tried to flee more than hinted at his guilt. But as of right now, Jake had no idea how they were going to build a murder case against him. Was this guy smart or stupid, and how wily an adversary was he going to prove to be? Would he have pre-prepared alibis for the killings? Would he be as cunning as Larry Mullins when it came to escaping justice?

And of course, there was always a direr possibility

Maybe we've got the wrong guy.

Jake told himself to be patient. He wouldn't know anything until he and Riley had a chance to interrogate Lutz at the Dalhart police station. He'd called ahead to alert Sheriff Quayle that they were bringing in a suspect. He'd also asked the sheriff to try to get search warrants, both for the utility van they'd seen parked in front of Mitch's Solutions and for Shawn Lutz's apartment. After Lutz's attempted escape, Jake didn't figure it would be hard to get a judge to sign off on a warrant.

With luck, maybe they'd wrap up this case tomorrow or even later today.

Then what?

Should this be Jake's last case, ever? Should he quit before his abilities dulled too seriously? He could think of just one good reason not to quit—at least not yet.

Riley.

One reason he'd chosen her as a protégé in the first place was so that someone could take his place at the BAU—someone with his own unique talents and abilities and instincts. He'd known from the day he first met her that she was definitely such a person.

But she was still so green—a "diamond in the rough," as he'd sometimes put it. How long would it be until she could work without his supervision? Riley was undisciplined, quick to take chances, often charging off in unexpected directions, putting herself in danger . . .

His ruminations were interrupted by the sound of Lutz's voice.

"Are we almost there?"

Jake chuckled. Lutz sounded for all the world like some kid getting impatient during a long family drive. So Jake said exactly what he'd always said to his own son years ago under similar circumstances.

"It won't be as long as it has been."

Indeed, Jake knew that they were already halfway to their destination.

It's nice to be sure of a little thing like that, he thought.

He wondered if he'd ever be so sure of the answers to those more complicated questions.

CHAPTER TWENTY TWO

Riley stood to one side in the interrogation room, watching and listening as Agent Crivaro asked Shawn Lutz one question after another.

This isn't going well, she thought, struggling with her feelings of discouragement.

Crivaro wasn't getting any answers—none at all. This was because Lutz had refused to say anything without a lawyer present. Sheriff Quayle had had no choice but to bring in a public defender, who had gotten here in a hurry and was sitting next to Lutz right now.

And the lawyer was doing his job all too well.

Every single time Crivaro asked Lutz a question, the lawyer would tell him the same thing.

"Don't answer that."

So far, Riley and Crivaro hadn't gleaned a single bit of useful information. She could tell that Crivaro was feeling even more demoralized than she was.

Still, Riley figured they had some cause for hope. Quayle had already obtained the search warrants they'd asked for, and cops were on their way right now to search that utility van and Lutz's apartment. With some luck, they'd turn up some valuable evidence.

Or better yet...

Maybe they'll find Sister Sandra while she's still alive.

The alternative was too horrible for Riley to even think about.

Right now Crivaro was asking Lutz about the two young girls and the missing nun, whether he had ever met them. Again and again, the lawyer told him not to say anything.

Crivaro let out a grunt of annoyance, then opened a folder with photos of the two dead girls and spread them out on the table in front of Lutz.

"Does this help your memory?" he asked.

Lutz's eyes widened.

"Now wait a minute," he said. "Wait just a minute. I didn't know—"

The lawyer interrupted sharply, "Shawn, don't say anything. Not one single word."

Lutz let out a surprised chuckle.

"But this is crazy," he said. "Does anybody really think—?"

"Not one word," the lawyer snapped.

Lutz turned to his lawyer and said, "But they're searching my place. They're going to find out for themselves—"

The lawyer said, "Shawn, if you don't keep quiet, I'm walking right out of here. You're going to have to find someone else to represent you. And in this county, you won't exactly have *la crème de la crème* to choose from. I'm the best you're going to get."

Lutz rolled his eyes, looking rather amused now.

"Okay, but this is stupid," he said. "I can't believe this is happening."

Crivaro kept pressing him about the girls, and where he'd been during the hours between when they'd disappeared and their bodies had been found. He asked where Lutz had been around the time Sister Sandra had gone missing. The lawyer kept telling him to keep his mouth shut, and Lutz kept complying.

Finally Crivaro fell silent. Riley could see his dismay in his face. He put the photos back into their folder and got up from his chair, apparently ready to abandon this interview.

Riley felt a flash of impatience.

We can't give up, she thought. *Not yet.*

But what could they do, short of forcibly pushing the lawyer out of the room?

Then she remembered something Mitch Brown had said back in his trailer. It had caught her attention at the time, but she'd almost forgotten about it.

Something to do with God.

Now she wondered if it might be important after all.

She leaned across the table toward the suspect.

"Hey, Shawn. I hear that God is dead. Is that right?"

His smile widened and his eyes sparkled.

"Where did you hear that?" he asked Riley.

"Oh, just around," Riley said, sitting in the chair where Crivaro had been sitting. "Do you think it's true?"

As Lutz opened his mouth to reply, his lawyer growled, "Shawn, I must have told you ten times already—"

Lutz interrupted with a hearty laugh.

"Yeah, yeah, yeah. I'm not supposed to talk. At all. I'm not deaf, you know. I heard you loud and clear. But hey, what's the harm of an innocent little theological discussion? I can't exactly incriminate myself chatting with this charming young lady about religion, can I?"

"Shawn, I mean it—" the lawyer said.

Lutz interrupted again, "I know, you'll walk out on me, I heard that too. Well, go ahead. When they search my house, they'll find out everything. Self-incrimination will be kind of a moot point then, won't it? So go ahead and leave. The door's right over there."

The lawyer growled and shook his head but didn't get up to leave.

Lutz smiled at Riley and said, "Now what was your question again?"

Riley shrugged and said, "I was just wondering whether God is really dead."

Lutz leaned back in his chair and said, "Well, what do *you* think? You seem like a smart girl. Do you go to church and say your prayers at night? I find that hard to believe, considering your line of work."

He nodded toward the folder under Crivaro's arm and added, "Those pictures alone ought to be enough to make an unbeliever out of you, Agent Sweeney. Or maybe you're too new to this job to start asking the obvious questions."

Riley almost shot back, *"I'm asking you the questions."*

But she knew it would be the wrong thing to say.

The trick right now was to distract him from the fact that this was still an interrogation—and that her seemingly irrelevant questions might have everything to do with the murders.

Yesterday, she'd had what felt like a flash of insight about the killer—that his choice of victims had something to do with religion. After all, Natalie and Kimberly had come from churchgoing families, and Sister Sandra was training for her first vows at a Catholic high school.

If she was right, pursuing the topic might draw him out.

"What kind of questions do you mean?" she asked.

Pointing to the pictures again, Lutz said, "For example, what kind of God would allow such terrible things to happen?"

To Riley's surprise, Crivaro spoke up.

"It's a dumb question to ask. I've been working at this job for a long time. If there *is* someone in charge of this crazy universe, he sure lets a lot of terrible stuff go on. I've seen people tortured and terrorized and maimed and hacked up by sick, sadistic monsters. So far, I've not seen one of those bastards get struck dead by a thunderbolt. But I've seen a lot of decent, innocent people suffer for no reason at all."

Lutz nodded and said, "Sounds like you and I might be on the same wavelength."

"All I know is, I've got a job to do," Crivaro said. "Somebody's got to bring some decency and justice to this crazy world."

"Oh, I think you know better than that, Agent Crivaro," Lutz said with a smile. "You know perfectly well that your job is completely futile. You're fighting the natural order of things. Decency and justice are just made-up ideas, like good and evil, or right and wrong."

Crivaro smirked and nodded, "Because, without God, all things are permitted, eh?"

Riley was truly startled now. She'd never heard Crivaro say anything quite like that before.

"Exactly," Lutz said. "Agent Crivaro, I've got real hopes for you. Maybe when we've cleared up this stupid misunderstanding, we can spend some time getting to know each other. You might be just the kind of person I keep looking for."

Crivaro grunted and said, "You sound like kind of a lonely guy, Shawn."

"Aren't you?" Lutz replied. "I can't imagine that you've got much in common with most people—including this girl here."

Riley felt her face flush with anger.

This "girl"?

He's got a hell of a nerve!

This girl just brought this guy in.

But she kept her anger to herself. She realized that Crivaro was taking his own approach to this suspect. More than that, he seemed to be establishing some kind of weird rapport with the suspect. Riley figured she'd better not interfere.

Crivaro chuckled cynically.

He said, "I've got to say, Shawn, I *am* kind of glad to make your acquaintance. It's hard to talk about this kind of stuff with regular folks."

"With the herd, you mean," Lutz said.

"Yeah, people are like cattle, aren't they?" Crivaro said. "They believe what they're told. They don't think for themselves. Not like you and me."

He nudged Riley, who got up and let him sit back down at the table. Then he leaned toward Lutz and spoke to him as if nobody else was in the room. Meanwhile, the lawyer just stared with his mouth hanging open, obviously wondering where this conversation could possibly be leading—and also whether he ought to put a stop to it.

Crivaro said, "You know, you might just be right about the futility of what I do. Just between you and me, I sometimes wonder if I'm just wasting my time as a lawman, and maybe I should just pack it in. Maybe I'm wrong and the bad guys are right."

Lutz laughed.

"There you go, talking about right and wrong again," he said. "There is no right or wrong. All we've got is our instincts and impulses. We should follow our instincts and ignore everything else. And if other people suffer—well, that's entirely irrelevant. The laws and morals of the herd are not meant for the likes of us. We're under no obligation to comply with them."

Crivaro shook his head and said to Lutz, "Yeah, it would be nice to get back to pure instinct. But it's hard to do, in a world where everybody's telling you what to do and how to live. I feel like I lost touch with my own instincts a long time ago."

Crivaro paused for a moment.

Then drumming his fingers on the table, he added, "I don't know what I want, Shawn. Deep down, I mean. All I know is that my job makes less and less sense to me. I want to find my way back to something more—well, primal, I guess."

Riley was starting to get alarmed now. As they kept talking, Crivaro didn't seem to be interrogating the suspect at all. Instead, he seemed almost to be confiding in him about his private doubts and longings.

Soon Lutz said something that really caught Riley's attention.

"That's why I keep looking for companions, kindred spirits, like-minded people."

Riley remembered a word Mitch Brown had used to describe him.

Persuasive.

Regarding the whole religion thing, Lutz seemed to have persuaded Mitch thoroughly. Mitch himself had said so.

"Don't guess I'll ever set foot in a church again, no matter how much my wife tries to drag me there."

And now Riley realized something about Lutz.

He's looking for converts.

Almost like some kind of missionary, he was trying to surround himself with people who believed and thought just like he did. Apparently he had succeeded with Mitch Brown. And right now, it seemed almost as though he was succeeding with Agent Crivaro.

Unless Crivaro is just playing along.

But surely Lutz couldn't succeed in persuading everybody. Riley tried to imagine how he might react to someone who didn't swallow his whole "God is dead" routine—someone who pushed back and tried to tell him he was wrong.

Suddenly the whole thing made horrible sense to Riley. Here Lutz was, preaching not only atheism but amorality, a life of pure instinct and impulse, with no regard for other people's feelings or even lives.

I'll bet his impulses aren't pretty, Riley thought.

She found it very easy to imagine him getting very angry who disagreed with him.

Was that what had happened with Natalie, and Kimberly, and Sister Sandra?

Were all three of them too religious to go along with him?

Had he murdered them to punish them?

Yes, that's it, she thought with a sharp tingle of certainty.

Riley wanted to get into the thick of the conversation Lutz was having with Crivaro. With this new insight, surely she could trip him up—maybe even get him to confess.

But before she could even think of what to say, the interrogation room door opened and Sheriff Quayle stepped inside.

He said, "Agents Crivaro and Sweeney—I need to have a word with you."

Crivaro looked annoyed to be interrupted. But he followed Riley and Quayle out of the booth into the adjoining room.

Riley could see that Quayle looked deeply alarmed.

He said, "My guys searched Lutz's place. They found something, all right. He's growing an impressive amount of marijuana in his basement."

Riley felt a jolt of surprise. But before she could wrap her mind about what this discovery might mean, Sheriff Quayle spoke again.

"I've got worse news. Another body has been found."

CHAPTER TWENTY THREE

Jake was concerned about his young partner's silence during the drive to the new crime scene. Even as he kept his attention on following Sheriff Quayle's car, he couldn't help wondering how Riley was taking the news of another victim. So far during the drive, she hadn't said a word.

Finally, in a broken, stammering voice, she said, "Agent Crivaro...do you think...?"

Her voice faded, but Jake knew what she wanted to ask.

Might this new victim be Sister Sandra?

"I don't know, Riley," Jake said. "Even Sheriff Quayle doesn't know. All he knows is that another body has been found. We'll just have to see."

His words were of no comfort, and he knew it.

And the truth was, he was plenty anxious about that himself.

Just yesterday, he'd been sure that Sister Sandra was just a runaway, not an abduction victim at all. He might well have been wrong. If she had been murdered, what did that say about his judgment?

He stifled a discouraged groan. Ever since they had started working on this case, he'd been badgering Riley about whether she was up to the job.

But what about me?

Am I up to it?

Trying to shake off his apprehension, he decided that both he and Riley needed to talk about something else.

"What did you think about our suspect?" he asked.

In an expressionless monotone, Riley said, "We know he was growing pot in his basement. When he first saw us back at that trailer, maybe he thought that was why we were after him."

"Yeah, and maybe that was why he ran," Jake said. "But we can't be sure of that. We can't be sure of anything, the way his lawyer keeps him from answering our questions about alibis and such."

"He sure talked a lot, though," Riley said. "To you, anyway."

Jake grunted and said, "Yeah, I guess I've got a way of drawing out that kind of a guy. It was pretty easy to figure out his worldview—one part Nietzsche, one part Dostoevsky."

Riley gave Jake a slightly surprised look.

Jake said, "Hey, don't look at me like I'm supposed to be some illiterate stooge. I've read some books, you know. Nietzsche's the philosopher who said that God is dead. Dostoevsky wrote novels about what people would do if they really believed that. He figured they'd be capable of any sort of crime, including murder. 'Without God, all things are permitted,' he said."

"Is that what you believe?" Riley asked.

Jake was taken aback by the question.

He forced a laugh and said, "Come on, you know me better than that."

"He sure seemed to think you were on his wavelength," Riley said.

Jake shook his head and said nothing for a few seconds. The truth was, he was still unsettled by that interview—not just by things Lutz had said, but things he'd heard himself saying.

"Riley, this job really gets under your moral skin after a while," Jake said. "It's only natural that you start suspecting the worst about human nature. But you also start wondering about the whole damned universe. Who's in charge, anyway? And why does he—or she—let so many terrible things happen in the world?"

Jake thought for a moment, and then added, "You should read some Dostoevsky, you know. In a way, he was one hell of a forensic psychologist. You can learn stuff from him that you can't get out of any textbooks."

Another silence fell between them.

"So what do *you* think about Shawn Lutz?" Riley asked.

Jake thought for a moment.

Then he said, "Well, aside from being a pseudo-intellectual, he's also a sociopath, and a narcissist, and more than a bit of a bullshit artist. And if you want to know whether he's capable of murder..."

Jake shrugged and added, "I'd say maybe, yeah."

Jake followed Sheriff Quayle's car as he turned off the main highway onto a gravel country road. After about a mile, a group of parked vehicles came into sight—a couple of police cars and a medical examiner's van. There was no shoulder along there, so the cars pretty much blocked the road—not that it looked like there was ever much traffic this way.

Quayle pulled over, and Jake parked right behind him. He and Riley got out of the car and followed Quayle over to a group of cops. The county sheriff came forward to meet them.

The sheriff said to Quayle, "This looks like your serial killer's work. Since you put out the APB to warn the public, I called you as soon as I found out about it."

Quayle asked him, "Who found the body?"

"It was a jogger out running with his dog a while ago," the sheriff said. Then he pointed to a patch of tall weeds and added, "The dog got interested in something in the grass over there. That's where the jogger found her."

Jake looked where the sheriff was pointing. Standing in some tall weeds were the ME and his team. They were taking photographs.

As he and Riley and Quayle followed the sheriff out into the weeds, Jake realized that his pulse was racing. He wasn't sure why. He'd visited hundreds of crime scenes before, and had long since gotten inured to the sight of a corpse. Why was he feeling so agitated this time?

Soon the body came into view, and Jake realized that his anxiety was all too well justified.

He heard the sheriff ask, "Do you have any idea who the victim is?"

"Yeah," Jake said. "It's Sister Sandra Hobson, a teacher at Magdalene High School."

Jake knew there could be no mistake. The victim was dressed in a white habit and a black and white wimple.

But she didn't look real somehow. Lying there in the thin snow with her hands crossed on her chest, she looked utterly peaceful, like some fairytale princess awaiting the kiss of a handsome young prince to bring her back to life. Even the bruise on her neck looked somehow ornamental, not like something caused by a brutal act of strangulation.

Jake barely listened as Quayle, the sheriff, and the ME talked about the body and how it was found. One question was uppermost in Jake's mind.

Did Shawn Lutz do this?

It wasn't impossible, at least according to the time frame as he understood it. They'd arrested Lutz just a couple of hours ago, but Sister Sandra had gone missing the night before last and had been left here last night.

They needed to find out where Lutz had been during those periods of time. In fact, they'd have to find out where he'd been over a wide range of hours, since all of the victims had been abducted well before they were killed. Lutz seemed to be the independent kind of guy who could do whatever he wanted at whatever hour he wanted to. He just could be the serial killer they were looking for.

But still . . .

Jake tried to imagine Shawn Lutz bringing Sister Sandra's body here, laying her gently among these weeds and arranging her so perfectly. Jake remembered Lutz's smirking, superior attitude—and most of all, his utter contempt for any notion of right or wrong. Could he have created the weirdly reverent spectacle Jake was looking upon right now?

Jake searched his mind for an answer. But his normally keen instincts just weren't kicking in.

Maybe Riley can get a better idea.

But just as he was about to turn and ask her, he felt a heavy weight on his shoulder. He quickly realized that Riley had fallen against him and was clinging to him for support.

"Riley! What's the matter?" he said.

But Riley didn't reply. She'd gone deathly pale, and her eyes were rolling back under their lids. Jake managed to catch her before she fainted dead away.

He held her up and lifted her chin and whispered, "Come on, kid. Let's get you away from here."

She nodded mutely and allowed him to start leading her away.

Jake heard the ME's voice calling after him.

"What do you want us to do with the body?"

Jake knew there was no point in preserving the crime scene exactly in its current state. He was already sure that this killing was exactly like the others.

He turned toward the ME and said, "You can load her up and take her away."

As the ME started giving orders to his team, Jake began to lead Riley toward their borrowed car. He was anxious that she not collapse in full view of the cops and the ME's team. He managed to get her into the back seat of their vehicle and climbed in beside her.

"Put your head down," Jake said to her in a gentle voice. "Breathe deep and slow."

Riley obeyed, holding her head against her knees for a minute or so. Then she jerked back and gasped, as if she were suddenly bursting through the surface of water after being submerged and holding her breath for too long.

"It's my fault," she cried out in a desperate voice. "She's dead because of me."

"It's not your fault," Jake said.

"It is," Riley said, starting to sob. "I let them down. I let both of them down."

Jake was momentarily confused.

Both of them?

Then he realized...

Heidi Wright.

The sight of Sister Sandra's body had reawakened that other recent trauma.

Jake began to sputter and try to reassure her that neither death was her fault—that she'd had no choice but to kill Heidi, and someone else entirely was responsible for what had happened to Sister Sandra. But Riley wouldn't listen.

"They deserved better," she sobbed.

"Heidi was a killer," he reminded her.

"She was a human being, just like Sandra. They both deserved to live. They're dead because of me. And more people are going to die. And we don't know how to stop them from dying."

"We don't know that," Jake said. "We've got a suspect in custody."

"He didn't kill anybody and you know it," Riley said.

Jake couldn't argue with her. He knew she might well be right. As distraught as she was, her instincts were still working better than his. And even he hadn't been able to imagine Shawn Lutz carrying out this murder.

Jake tried to put his arms around Riley, but she pushed him sharply away.

"I told you," she said angrily. "You didn't listen."

Jake felt as though his breath had been knocked out of him.

She's right, he thought.

He remembered how hard he'd been on her for insisting that Sister Sandra had been abducted—especially when she'd wanted to return to the Magdalene campus that night.

I could have gone with her, Jake thought.

Instead he'd thrust the car keys at her.

"Go ahead, knock yourself out," he'd said.

He was seized with shame at his terrible mistake.

How could I have been so wrong? he wondered.

Had he let his own miserable years in a Catholic school affect his judgment? Had that been why he'd been so convinced that Sister Sandra had simply run away—because he couldn't imagine anyone choosing to live the life she'd so wholeheartedly chosen?

Worst of all, if he'd gone with Riley last night, could they have solved this case once and for all?

Could they have rescued Sister Sandra before she was killed?

Jake's thoughts were in turmoil, but Riley seemed to be calming herself.

"I'm sorry, Agent Crivaro," she said. "You were right to doubt me. I just can't deal with this. I don't think I can ever work on a murder case ever again. I'll never be any good as an agent. I just can't do it. It's time for me to go home."

Jake took hold of her hand and squeezed it and said nothing.

He felt deeply exhausted, and his self-confidence was gone.

It's almost funny, he thought.

Ever since they'd flown out here the day before yesterday, he'd been trying to get Riley to decide whether she was up to working on this case.

And now that she'd finally decided...

I can't let her go back.

He knew he couldn't solve this case without her help.

CHAPTER TWENTY FOUR

L arissa Billham sipped on her coffee and looked at her watch again.

Where is he? she wondered.

He'd said he was just going to the restroom, but that had been a good many minutes ago. As she sat alone at the table in the bustling Howard Johnson's, she wondered—had she put him off somehow, maybe even offended him?

Or had he simply decided he didn't like her and just taken off?

That would be rude of him, of course.

But with a sigh she realized—it would fit with her meager experiences with male behavior.

Maybe this whole thing was a mistake, she thought.

But she was thirty-two years old, and a kind of desperation had been coming over her lately. She felt like it was time to make a major change in her life. She hadn't so much as been out on a date in eight or nine years. And those long-ago experiences had soured her on men. As the old saying put it . . .

"They're all after just one thing."

And she'd never been ready for that "thing" back in those days—certainly not with the guys in question. In fact, she'd never done that "thing" at all. She'd given up on men altogether—until now.

She wondered—was she making a mistake?

Larissa blushed as she remembered how her friend Penny had reacted when she'd let the truth slip to her during a coffee break at work a couple of weeks ago.

"You're a virgin?" Penny had exclaimed, so loudly that Larissa was afraid someone else would hear her. *"What the hell's the matter with you? Are you going to spend the rest of your life trying to be Doris Day?"*

Penny had badgered her about it during the days that followed. Larissa just had to get laid, she said—*"by any means necessary."*

And Larissa had some pretty vulgar ideas of what those "means" might be.

A year or so ago, Larissa would have shrugged off Penny's entreaties. But that quiet desperation that had been creeping up inside her seemed to be getting stronger every day. She'd done nothing with her adult life so far except be an efficient and perfectly capable paralegal at Colville & Bean.

It was time for a change.

It was time for an adventure.

She wasn't looking for sex, she kept telling herself—just the kind of companionship she'd been denying herself all these years.

Of course she knew that sex might wind up being part of that package. The prospect scared her a little. But nobody ever said adventures shouldn't be a little scary. And anyway, it was about time for a change in that department as well.

A server came by the table and asked, "Are you ready to order?"

Larissa said, "No, I'm waiting for my . . . friend to come back."

The server smiled tensely and headed off toward another table. Larissa understood the server's attitude from when she'd waited tables herself many years ago. She'd learned way back then that a server had to stay in constant motion during a frantic lunch shift like this.

"Run and gun," they'd called it in those days.

Larissa looked at her watch again.

I'll give him three more minutes, she thought. *Then I'll leave.*

It was noon here at the Howard Johnson's, and the place was packed, and the servers were extremely busy.

What a crazy time and place for a date, she thought.

She remembered how this whole thing had been set up. She'd had no intention of striking up some kind of relationship "by any means necessary." She wanted to be sensible about it—and safe. She didn't want to wind up with the same kind of guy who had put her off guys in the first place.

One day recently while waiting her turn in a hair salon, she'd run across a monthly newsletter entitled *Wholesome Ways.* She'd found it to be rather charming—full of non-denominational advice on how to live a clean, moral life. It seemed like a quaint relic of an earlier era, all about the importance nuclear families and abstinence before marriage. It included recipes, games, vacation ideas—and also personals ads, most of them from people looking for like-minded people to date.

She'd come up with the clever idea of putting a dating ad in *Wholesome Ways* herself. She was sure that it would guarantee that whoever answered it wouldn't be another creep on the make. It would be someone with intentions that were more . . .

Well, virtuous.

But she didn't want a guy who was so virtuous that he'd bore her to death. He needed to be open to . . .

Possibilities.

The ads from women typically stipulated that they weren't interested in sex, just affection and companionship and common values. She knew she had to word her own ad a little differently. So she came up with something she hoped would work:

32 year-old attractive female, lives in Boneau, KY
Unattached since, well, forever.
Hoping to change all that with an attractive, intelligent, gentle, considerate male who respects boundaries.

She'd signed the ad with the name "Annette." She'd quickly gotten a response on the newsletter's message board from a guy who called himself Nick, who lived in the nearby town of Sigmont. After they'd exchanged a handful of messages, Nick had struck her as a charming guy.

Nick had been coy about going into any details about his past relationships via email. But he was just a few years older than Larissa, and she got the distinct impression that he, too, had never been in a long-term relationship.

We'll be on equal footing, she'd thought.

But where and when to meet for the first time had proven to be a whole different issue. Boneau was full of gossipy people, and Larissa dreaded being seen with a date anywhere in town. Nick seemed to feel exactly the same way about Sigmont.

He'd come up with an amusing suggestion that sounded like it would suit both of them. They'd meet for lunch at Howard Johnson's just off the nearby interstate. It was hardly a romantic setting for their first date, but the chances of either of them being seen by anybody they knew there were just about nil.

Larissa had cheerfully agreed to the idea, and now here she was.

In a curious way, it really did feel like the ideal place to meet. Although the restaurant was packed and busy, there wasn't a single familiar face anywhere. Most, if not all of the patrons were just passing through on the interstate. Not only had Larissa never seen any of them ever before, she was all but certain never to see any of them ever again.

It really felt quite perfect in its way—even oddly private, despite the ongoing bustle of activity.

But it was starting to look like things weren't going at all as she had hoped.

She looked at her watch again.

It's time to give up, she decided.

She felt lucky that they hadn't ordered yet. When they'd arrived, a server had asked if she and Nick wanted anything to drink while they decided what to order, and they'd both asked for coffee. If she left here right now, she could simply leave enough cash to pay for both of their coffees and also leave a nice tip.

She put some money on the table. But just when she was putting on her jacket and getting ready to leave, she heard a voice.

"Say—you're not trying to get away from me, are you?"

She turned and saw the man who called himself Nick smiling down at her. As she had when she'd first met him a little while ago, she melted a bit at the sight of his smiling face. He was a much more handsome man than she'd dared to hope for.

Larissa stammered, "Oh, no, I just ... wondered ..."

Nick sat down again across from her.

"I know, I was gone for longer than I expected. I'm sorry to have kept you waiting. I had to make a phone call. Business, of course."

Larissa took her jacket back off and picked up the money from the table.

Then she looked at Nick curiously. Judging from his clothes and grooming, she figured he must be fairly prosperous. But neither of them had mentioned their jobs during their communications so far.

She asked shyly, "So—what *is* your business?"

Nick ducked his head and smiled sheepishly, as if he didn't want to reply.

"You go first," he said. "Tell me about yourself."

She wondered whether this might be a good time for both of them to come clean about their real names. But somehow she didn't feel ready for that.

Instead she laughed and said, "I guess you could say I'm in the divorce business."

Nick raised his eyebrows in surprise.

Larissa added, "I'm a paralegal for Colville & Bean."

Nick nodded knowingly.

"Oh, yes," he said. "The divorce law firm in Boneau."

"That's right," Larissa said. "You'd be surprised at what a thriving business we do, even in this part of the country."

Nick shook his head and sighed.

"Oh, I'm not surprised at all," he said. "The decay of family values is spreading simply everywhere."

Larissa felt a twinge of unease at the moralistic tone in his voice. Meanwhile, she noticed the server making another pass at their table. The server looked at them and obviously sensed that they were in mid-conversation and still hadn't made up their minds what to order, so he moved right on again.

"Okay, it's your turn," she said, forcing a smile. "What do you do?"

Nick said, "Oh, it's nothing interesting. The truth is, I'm still very curious about *you*."

Larissa didn't know whether to feel flattered or uneasy.

Is there something he doesn't want to tell me? she wondered.

Nick paused for a moment. Then he looked her in the eyes and said, "Please believe me, I'm not in the habit of doing this. I've never answered an ad like that before. But yours really caught my attention."

"How so?" Larissa asked.

Nick stroked his chin thoughtfully.

"Something about how it was worded, I guess," he said. "You wrote that you'd been 'unattached forever.' Does that mean...?"

His voice trailed off, but Larissa could tell what he meant to ask.

And she felt distinctly uneasy now.

She stammered, "I–I'm not sure I want to talk about—you know."

Nick continued, "It's just that... well, most ads in that particular publication are clearer on the subject."

Larissa's mind flashed back to some of the ads she'd seen in *Wholesome Ways*. She knew that Nick was right. Even the dating ads typically indicated an intention to "wait until marriage."

Her own ad had been deliberately unclear.

"I don't mean to make you uncomfortable," Nick said.

Well, that's what you're doing, Larissa thought.

At the same time, it seemed rather silly of her to feel this way. After all, this man had answered a dating ad that she'd made public. Didn't he have a right to ask some personal questions—even about her sex life?

Maybe, she thought. Still, she felt troubled and confused.

He leaned across the table toward her.

He said, "There was something else you wrote in the ad—'Hoping to change all that.' That worried me. Hoping to change *what* exactly? Are you thinking about...?"

Larissa found herself holding her breath as the words hung unspoken in the air.

Nick shook his head sadly.

He said, "Annette, do you realize how rare it is for someone to get to be your age and still hold on to that—innocence? Have you really thought this through? It's a precious thing you're thinking about giving up. And once it's gone, you'll never get it back again."

Larissa didn't like the turn this conversation had taken.

She said, "Nick, what's this all about? I mean, are we really here on a date?"

"Of course," Nick said. "What else could it be?"

Larissa shrugged and said, "Well, it sounds like you're kind of..."

She stopped herself from finishing her thought.

"... *kind of lecturing me about morality.*"

But from Nick's expression, he clearly knew that she meant to say.

He let out a self-critical groan and rolled his eyes.

"Oh, I'm doing it again, aren't I?" he said. "I don't mean to get all moralistic. It's just something I do at inappropriate moments. I'm really very sorry."

Somewhat to Larissa's relief, his apology sounded perfectly sincere.

"It's all right," she said.

"Perhaps we should order some lunch," Nick said.

Pushing her coffee cup aside, Larissa said, "No, I'd really rather not, if it's all the same to you."

She searched for the right words for a few seconds.

Then she said, "Look, I think I made a mistake. Taking out that ad, I mean. It was . . . well, it wasn't like me at all. *This* isn't like me at all. I really shouldn't be here."

"I'm really sorry," Nick said again.

"No, please don't feel bad, this isn't your fault. It was kind of you to answer my ad, and I'm sorry to disappoint you, but . . ."

Nick tilted his head sympathetically.

"Oh, I understand, don't worry," he said. "I understand how you feel. And the last thing I want is to be pushy. Maybe we should just call it a day and get back to our regular lives."

Larissa sighed with relief.

"I'm so glad you understand," she said, reaching into her purse.

Nick took out his own wallet and said, "No, please, let me pay for this."

He put a rather generous amount cash on the table. They put on their jackets, and Nick walked her outside to her car—a used car that she'd bought cheaply to save money. She and Nick shook hands chastely, and then he walked away.

It occurred to her that they'd never gotten around to telling each other their real names.

Maybe it's just as well, she thought.

She got into her car and tried to start it.

The ignition let out an agonized rattle.

She groaned aloud and tried again. The same thing happened.

She was surprised and annoyed. This car had been dependable since she'd bought it, even on some really cold days. Why wouldn't it start now?

Just not my lucky day, I guess, she thought.

But what was she going to do?

Then came a knock on the driver's window. When she saw that it was Nick, she rolled her window down.

"It sounds like you're having some trouble," he said. "Can I help?"

"I'm not sure," she said. "Do you have jumper cables?"

"Try starting it again," Nick said.

She did, and this time the ignition barely made a sound.

Nick shook his head and said, "I don't know what your problem is, but it's not the battery. Jumper cables wouldn't do any good. You need to get towed somewhere to get it worked on."

Larissa looked around and didn't see a service station nearby. She fought down a cry of frustration.

"I don't have time for this," she said. "I've got to get back to work."

Nick said, "I understand, but surely I can help." He pointed and added, "There's a gas station about a quarter of a mile that way. I'll drive you over there and you can tell them your problem, and they'll send a tow truck."

"But I don't have time to wait for it to get repaired," Larissa said. "I'll be late getting back to work."

"That's okay, I'll drive you to Boneau," Nick said. "You can come back and get the car whenever it's ready."

Larissa could hardly believe her ears.

"Oh, no, I can't ask you to do that," she said. "Boneau's much too far out of your way."

"No, it's all right," Nick said with a charming smile. "The rest of my day is pretty much free. And it seems like the least I can do after...well, disappointing you."

In a voice brimming with gratitude, Larissa said, "That's more than kind of you. Thank you. Thank you so much."

She got out of her car and followed him across the parking lot toward a white utility van. She was a bit surprised to see that such a well-dressed man was driving a rather unattractive vehicle. But she didn't much care, as long as he was going to give her a ride.

"Sorry about the company vehicle," he explained. "But it runs just fine."

As they walked around the back of the vehicle toward the passenger's side, Larissa noticed that the sliding door along the side was partly open.

That's odd, she thought.

She was about to ask why it was open when she felt a powerful, vise-like hand on her shoulder.

Larissa Billham knew right then and there that she was in terrible danger.

CHAPTER TWENTY FIVE

Eyes closed, Riley leaned her head against the passenger's window of their borrowed car. She wasn't paying any attention to where they were going. She just assumed that Crivaro was driving them back to Dalhart, where she would fetch her belongings in the motel, make her way to the airport, and catch the first flight back to DC.

And it's a good thing, too.

She remembered what she'd told him at the crime scene.

"I'll never be any good as an agent. I just can't do it. It's time for me to go home."

Crivaro hadn't said a word in disagreement. In fact, he hadn't said a word at all. It seemed pretty obvious that he agreed with her.

And how can I blame him?

She didn't think that he held her responsible for Sister Sandra's death. After all, he had rejected Riley's argument that the nun had been abducted.

Riley and Crivaro had both failed Sister Sandra.

But she was sure that Crivaro wasn't ignoring one painfully obvious fact. Riley simply didn't have the psychological resilience for this job. She'd been a wreck ever since she'd killed Heidi Wright.

She wondered—would she have fared better if she'd followed everybody's advice and talked to a therapist before coming back to work? She doubted it.

Riley felt as though something inside her had snapped for good. All the therapy in the world wasn't likely to help.

I'm through.

She might as well go back to Quantico and turn in her badge and her gun.

Anyway, she wondered if maybe there was an upside. Her job had been driving a wedge between her and Ryan. Maybe now they could patch things up once and for all.

But she felt a deep disappointment even so. Was she going to spend the rest of her life being Ryan's idea of a good wife? It didn't seem like much to look forward to.

Riley's eyes snapped open as the car slowed and rattled across a train track.

She was surprised to recognize some of the modest buildings that lined the streets.

"We're in Boneau," she said.

"Yep," Crivaro said.

"I thought we were heading back to Dalhart."

"Not yet," Crivaro grunted. "We've got some business to take care of here first."

"But where are we going?" Riley asked.

"I'll know it when I see it," Crivaro said.

He turned off the main street onto a side street.

Then he pulled the car to a stop and said, "Aha. That's just the kind of place I'm looking for."

Riley's eyes widened with confusion. Crivaro was parking in front of a run-down-looking bar called Bobby's Bait House. It was housed in what almost looked like a condemned building. But the place was open, all right. A neon beer sign was flickering in the window.

"Come on, let's go inside," Crivaro said.

"But why?" Riley asked.

"Why not?" Crivaro said.

They got out of the car and walked on into the dank, dimly lit bar, where the jukebox was playing a scratchy record of a song from a couple of decades back. It was the kind of dive that could be anywhere. The only reminder that they were near the banks of a majestic river was a stained and faded image of a paddlewheel riverboat on the wall.

Riley followed Crivaro straight to the bar, where he ordered bourbon with ice for both of them.

As the bartender poured their drinks, Riley said, "Aren't we on duty?"

Crivaro chuckled gruffly and said, "Not at the moment, we're not."

They picked up their drinks, and Riley followed Crivaro over to a booth with tattered, black vinyl upholstery.

They sat down, and Crivaro looked all around with a satisfied expression.

He said, "This place pretty well suits our mood, don't you think?"

"I don't understand," Riley said.

Crivaro shook his head and said, "Riley, when you've been doing this job for as long as I have, you learn something about your own goddamn limits. It can be like hitting a brick wall. You learn to respect those limits, not try to push past them. And sometimes that means letting yourself fall the hell to pieces once in a while."

Crivaro leaned across the table toward her.

He said almost in whisper, "I know you've hit that wall. What you might not know is—I've hit it too."

Riley's mouth fell open. She didn't know what to say.

Crivaro added, "First of all, I've got to tell you—you're not going back to Quantico. Not now. Not until we finish this case. Because . . ."

Crivaro's voice faded for a moment.

"I'm burnt out, Riley," he said. "I've got nothing. That nun's dead because I didn't trust your instincts. And I damn well should have trusted your instincts, because my own are shot to hell. I think we both need to talk."

Crivaro stared at the tabletop for a moment.

Then he raised his glass and said, "Here's to the brick wall we've just smashed into. And maybe to chasing away a few inner demons."

Riley obediently clicked her glass against his.

They took small sips from their drinks and sat in silence for a moment.

Then Crivaro said, "When you and I were flying out here, I told you about the Magrette bank robbery, and how it led to my first gunfight. And the lesson of my story was—well, that it didn't have much of a lesson, at least not for you. I didn't feel a thing when I killed the leader of that bank robbery gang. In fact, I didn't even know I'd shot him, because I'd been shooting blindly every which way. I didn't know I'd hit anybody until I saw him lying dead on the ground. And it sure didn't haunt me over the years."

Crivaro crinkled his brow in thought.

Then he said, "But one particular moment of that day still sticks in my memory. I can remember the very first bullet that whizzed by my head when the gunfight was just getting underway. I remember it like it was yesterday—or even just a few minutes ago."

Riley felt an unexpected jolt of agitation.

Suddenly she remembered the whistling buzz of a bullet whipping right past her head—the first shot that anyone had ever fired deliberately at her.

"I had that happen too," Riley said.

Crivaro asked, "Has it been nagging at you? Have you been flashing back to it?"

Riley squinted with thought.

"No," she said. "I'd forgotten all about it. Until just now."

Crivaro shook his head and said, "Riley, I doubt that very much. It's been just below the surface of your thoughts this whole time. You've been repressing it. And it's been bothering you a lot more than you realize."

Riley stared at the tabletop for a moment, feeling terrified and yet strangely relieved to let that terrible moment come back to her.

Then she said, "I was just two or three inches away from death."

Crivaro nodded and said, "And *now* how do you feel about it?"

The memory of that whizzing bullet was echoing through Riley's consciousness.

Riley said, "I feel like . . . this moment, us talking together right now . . . it's not real. It's not happening. What's real is that bullet."

Then with a slight gasp, she added, "My *death* is what seems real."

"And your life doesn't," Crivaro said.

"It doesn't, no," Riley said. "It feels like my life is some sort of . . ."

She paused, looking for the right word.

"Mistake?" Crivaro said.

Riley felt an eerie calmness starting to settle over her.

"Yeah, that's it," Riley said. "Like I'm not supposed to be here."

Crivaro looked at her sympathetically.

He said, "Riley, if you survive in this job, if you keep beating the odds and don't get hit by one of those bullets or get killed in any one of a million possible ways, you'll get this same weird feeling over and over again. And with that feeling can come . . ."

He paused, letting Riley search for the right word.

It came to her right away.

"Guilt," she said.

"That's right," Crivaro said. "We both know you've been feeling guilty about Heidi Wright. But maybe you haven't come to grips with the starkness of it, the either/or nature of what happened."

Riley nodded slowly.

"One of us had to die," she said. "Heidi or me. I thought I was feeling guilty for killing Heidi. But really, I'm feeling guilty for..."

She gasped slightly.

"For being alive," she said.

"Yeah. And believe me, you're going to feel that way again and again," Crivaro said. "But you can't repress it. You've got to come to terms with it, even when you're in the midst of it. You've got to keep telling yourself, being alive is nothing to feel guilty about."

Riley felt as though a weight was starting to lift from her mind.

But it wasn't gone yet.

Something else was troubling her, and she knew she had to bring it out into the open.

Now she found herself remembering again Heidi's eerily contented smile as she'd aimed her gun at Riley.

And then . . .

It came back to her all too clearly.

She said to Crivaro, "When I shot Heidi, I never *decided* to do it. I remember feeling somehow outside of myself. It was like I *watched* myself raise my weapon, or rather watched somebody else raise my weapon, then felt somebody else pull the trigger. It was like someone else did it, not me."

Crivaro smiled knowingly.

"That 'someone else' is real, Riley," he said. "And you'd better be grateful for it. It's the part of you that wants to stay alive, even when the rest of you feels ready to give up. It's the part of you that's trained to stay alive. And like I just said..."

Riley finished his thought, "Being alive is nothing to feel guilty about."

Riley felt as though everything was changing, becoming clearer—as if even this dimly lit bar was becoming brighter.

But this clarity seemed to be stirring up as many questions as answers.

Just as one of those questions was stirring to the surface, Crivaro's phone rang. Seeing that the call was from Sheriff Quayle, Crivaro put the call on speakerphone.

Quayle asked, "Are you two still in Boneau?"

Riley and Crivaro exchanged amused glances.

"Yes," Crivaro said, not offering to tell the sheriff exactly where they were at the moment.

"Good," Quayle said. "I'm almost back to Dalhart, but I just got a call from the county sheriff over there. He says we've got another missing persons report from right there in Boneau. The sheriff's out at the medical examiner's office. You guys are probably the closest to the caller."

Riley felt a tingle of alarm.

Crivaro told Quayle, "Sure, we can check it out."

Quayle continued, "I'm not sure if it's anything real yet. This seems like too soon for our killer to be making another abduction."

Crivaro replied, "He could be changing his MO. Anyhow, we've been moving way too slowly on these tips."

"This one came from the Colville & Bean law office," Quayle said. He gave them an address on Main Street, which sounded to Riley like it must be just a couple of blocks away from the bar.

"We'll be right there," Crivaro said, then ended the call.

As she and Crivaro were getting up from the table to leave, Riley noticed the drinks still on the table. She was pretty sure she'd only taken a sip or two, and that Crivaro had done the same.

"Hey, leave those drinks alone," Crivaro laughed as he was putting on his jacket. "We're on duty, remember?"

He wagged his finger at her and added, "And that's the last free psychiatric advice you're getting from me. You need to see a shrink when you get back to Quantico. I mean it."

Riley smiled as she followed him out the door to the car. Her senior partner might not think of himself as a therapist, but Riley doubted that any real shrink could have Crivaro's insights into the life and psyche of a BAU agent.

Still, she wished they'd had time to talk about one more thing.

She was still troubled by last night's dream, and the delight she'd taken in gunning down Larry Mullins.

Might she really wind up like that someday? Eager to kill?

Crivaro was a tough guy, but he'd managed to hold on to his humanity.

What about me? Riley thought.

Could she keep hunting monsters without becoming one herself?

CHAPTER TWENTY SIX

It was just a few blocks from Bobby's Bait House to the law office, and Riley thought they might as well have walked. The day was sunny and bright, and she could actually glimpse the Mississippi that flowed past the edge of town. But this was no time for admiring the scenery. If another woman really was missing, she knew they might not have a minute to spare.

We just can't lose a fourth victim, she thought.

Crivaro parked on Main Street in front of an old brick building with a false front. The main floor was occupied by a real estate office with images in a window picturing a more elegant lifestyle than Riley had seen any signs of here so far.

Hanging outside a second doorway was a sign that read:

Colville & Bean
River Work Injury and Family Law

"What do you suppose 'river work injury' means exactly?" Riley asked Crivaro as they got out of the car and walked toward the building.

Crivaro said, "A lot of the work along the Mississippi can be pretty hazardous. Guys who work on docks and riverboats and barges get hurt pretty regularly in accidents of one kind or another. Somebody needs to stand up for those workers against their employers. That's where lawyers come in."

With a slight scoff, Crivaro added, "Of course, in a town like this these days, 'family law' might be a more thriving business than river accidents."

Riley nodded and muttered, "I'll bet they get divorce and custody and child support cases left and right."

The street door opened onto a wooden staircase, so Riley and Crivaro climbed the steps to a landing at the top. The single door there again announced

Colville & Bean. When they opened the law office door, a woman was waiting for them, pacing anxiously in a reception area.

"Oh, thank God," she said, wringing her hands. "You must be the FBI agents the sheriff said were on their way. I'm worried sick. You've got to do something."

Agent Crivaro said a few calming words to the woman and asked her to sit down and give them all the details. As the woman guided them to a sofa and chairs there in the reception area, Riley observed that the lawyers' offices were in the back. Their names were posted on the frosted glass panels in two separate doors. Off to one side of the reception area, an old-fashioned wooden swinging gate set apart another office space.

They all sat down in the reception area, and the woman introduced herself as Penny Mack, the receptionist. Penny was a hearty-looking woman in her late thirties, with cheerfully dyed hair and wearing a colorful dress.

Crivaro looked around at the quiet office.

"Where's everybody else?" he asked.

"There's just me right now," Penny said. "Devon and Josh—our two law-yers—are over in Rimrock having a long lunch meeting. I told Larissa this would be a good time for her to . . ."

She paused, and then said with a gasp of despair, "Oh, I'm afraid I've done something awful."

"Please explain," Riley said in a gentle voice. "Who is Larissa? What do you think might have happened to her?"

"Larissa is our paralegal," Penny said. Pointing past the wooden gate, she added, "She works at that desk over there."

"Where did she go?" Crivaro asked.

"I wish I knew exactly," Penny said in a choked voice. "On a date, anyway. Larissa is a workaholic, and she's awfully shy and withdrawn. So I encouraged her—kind of pushed her, really—to meet somebody." She hesitated, then said, "Just wait a minute, I'll show you."

Penny got up and went through the swinging gate to the desk where Larissa worked. She found what she was looking for and brought it back to Crivaro and Riley.

Riley could see that it was some sort of newsletter. Penny was showing them the back, calling their attention to a small paragraph circled in ink.

Riley read the paragraph aloud.

32 year-old attractive female, lives in Boneau, KY
Unattached since, well, forever.
Hoping to change all that with an attractive, intelligent, gentle, considerate male who respects
boundaries.

"A personal ad," Crivaro commented. "She ran a personal ad?"

Penny explained, "It's hard to find good single men around here. She didn't know any guys who might be available. So I suggested that she put out a personal ad, maybe contact somebody in another town. That's what she did. And she got an email response pretty much right away."

"Who from?" Crivaro asked.

"I don't know," Penny said. "Larissa felt so weird about it, she wouldn't tell me his name. But she said they'd communicated, and he was nice, and he lived in a town nearby. I suggested that she set up a date for today, since Devon and Josh are out for a while and wouldn't notice she was gone. So that's what she did."

"How long has she been gone?" Crivaro asked.

"Since shortly before noon," Penny said. "She didn't tell me where she was going to meet the guy for lunch."

Crivaro looked at his watch and said, "She's only been gone two and a half hours. Are you sure—?"

Penny interrupted, "She said she'd be back at least an hour ago. And when Larissa says she'll be somewhere at a particular time, she really means it. You could set a clock by how she stays on schedule."

"Maybe this is the exception," Crivaro said. "Maybe the lunch date turned out really well. How do you know she didn't just decide to spend more time with this guy?"

"I tried to phone her," Penny said. "To find out if she was having a good time, and then again to find out when she was coming back. I didn't get any answer." Penny swallowed hard

Riley could see that there were tears in the receptionist's eyes as she continued, "Larissa is a wonderful person, she would never just run off. I've known her for years, and she's like a sister to me even though she's got an education and a good job and I never got much education at all. She doesn't have any actual family here. She worked hard for what she has."

Penny wrung her hands again and said, "I should have known better. I shouldn't have suggested it. We'd been hearing about these murders lately, and there was that warning a couple of days ago about going out at night alone. But I figured nothing bad would happen to her in the middle of the day."

Struggling not to burst into tears, Penny added, "What if I was wrong?"

Riley could see a trace of skepticism in Crivaro's eyes.

I can understand why, she thought.

Larissa had only been missing for an hour and a half—hardly any time at all under normal circumstances.

But Riley had a gut feeling that Penny's fears might be well-founded.

Crivaro kept talking to Penny, trying to get her to think of other reasons for her friend's disappearance, and why there might be no cause for alarm. Meanwhile, Riley picked up the newsletter, which was titled *Wholesome Ways.*

Something religious? Riley wondered.

Skimming through its pages, it appeared to be pretty nondenominational. But the content was definitely conservative, culturally speaking, and it promoted distinctly old-fashioned gender roles.

One column offered mothers advice on how to teach their daughters to cook, and another gave fathers advice on rugged sports activities they could share with their sons. Another article gave tips for how wives could keep their husbands from getting bored with them, and another suggested ways for husbands to surprise their wives with special treats.

The whole thing gave Riley the creeps. She found herself wondering what Ryan might think of it.

Is this the sort of life he's got in mind for us?

But she reminded herself to stay focused on the case. The newsletter definitely raised some peculiar questions. For example, why had Larissa chosen to put her personal ad in this particular publication?

Then Riley remembered what she'd told Crivaro yesterday—that she thought the killings were somehow about religion. The Dent family was all devoted churchgoers, and Hannah Booker had said that her daughter was religious...

And our latest victim is a nun.

Does that mean . . .?

Riley gently interrupted the questions Crivaro was asking.

"Penny, is your friend religious?"

"Oh, no," Penny said. "She isn't religious at all. I'm not either, and I know she's not because we've talked about it. It's not that we've got anything against religion, it's just that..." She shrugged. "Well, it's just not our thing, I guess."

Riley felt a bit deflated

So much for my religion theory.

Penny squinted at her and said, "Why do you ask?"

Pointing to the newsletter, "Well, this publication strikes me as something somebody religious might read."

"Oh," Penny said.

She looked away from Riley.

There's something she's not telling me, Riley thought.

Riley said, "Penny, why would she choose this particular newsletter for her personal ad?"

Penny forced a smile.

"Oh, I don't know," she said. "I thought it was a silly idea. But..." Penny glanced at Crivaro and added, "I shouldn't say anything. I'm sure it doesn't matter."

She doesn't want to talk about it in front of Crivaro, Riley thought.

Riley exchanged a meaningful look with her partner. He nodded, clearly getting the message that Riley needed to talk with Penny alone. He quietly slipped out the front door onto the stair landing.

Riley pointed to the ad.

She said to Penny, "I wonder if you could help me understand the wording of this ad. 'Unattached since forever,' she says. But she also says she's 'hoping to change all that' with a 'considerate male.' It's almost as if..."

Riley's voiced faded as she thought again about the victims—the two religious teenagers and the nun.

She felt the tingle of an approaching hunch.

She said, "Penny, is Larissa...sexually active?"

Penny shook her head.

Riley said, "Has she *ever* been sexually active?"

Blushing, Penny shook her head again.

Riley's tingle turned into a surge of realization.

Virgins, she thought. *He's killing virgins.*

155

CHAPTER TWENTY SEVEN

Riley knew that she had to convince Crivaro that her idea made sense. She hurried to the front door of the law office and called him back inside.

"I think he's killing virgins," she told him.

Crivaro crinkled his brow in thought as he listened to Riley explain her hunch.

Then he said, "You could be right. Sister Sandra would certainly have fit into that scenario. But we don't know about the two high school girls. I don't see what we can do with this theory without knowing for sure."

Riley stifled a discouraged moan.

How were they going to find out whether Natalie and Kimberly had ever had sex?

Meanwhile, Penny had been listening to everything they'd been saying.

"I want to help," Penny said. "Please tell me what I can do."

Riley thought quickly. If Larissa had really been abducted, then this was different from his other attacks. She was older and not a student or even connected with a school. He had apparently chosen her from a personal ad.

In spite of those changes, Riley still had the awful feeling that this was the same killer, striking again. And if he was changing his MO, how long would he wait before killing his new victim? Although he had kept the others alive for a day, they couldn't count on that now.

With all those unknowns, they didn't have time to go to the local police station and set to work there. They might not have a minute to lose. They needed to make this office their base of operations.

"We'll need your desk," Riley said to Penny.

The three of them sat around the desk to brainstorm about a course of action.

Riley said to Crivaro, "Do you remember when we paid a visit to Hannah Booker, Natalie's mother? What Hannah said about her daughter's murder?"

Crivaro scratched his chin.

"He said that God took Natalie away while she was 'still good.'"

Riley said, "It sure sounds like Hannah thought Natalie was a virgin."

Crivaro shrugged and said, "Yeah, but we can't exactly take Hannah's word for it. The woman's a basket case; she's got the emotions of a child. She probably had no idea whether her daughter was having sex or not. And anyway, we can't contact Hannah right now, since she doesn't have a phone."

Riley drummed her fingers on the desk.

"Maybe we can find out about Kimberly," she said.

"What, by calling her parents?" Crivaro said. "I wouldn't count on getting the truth from them either."

Riley said, "No, but we might be able to find out from Kimberly's best friend."

Crivaro looked at his watch.

"Goldie Dowling must still be in school," he said. "Maybe we can reach her when she gets home."

"We can't wait," Riley said. We've got to try to reach her at school."

Crivaro said to Penny, "We need the phone number for the high school in Dalhart."

Penny set right to work and found the number in less than a minute. A moment later, Riley, Crivaro, and Penny were all on speakerphone with the school principal. The principal sounded skeptical when Crivaro and Riley introduced themselves as BAU agents.

He said, "You're asking me to haul one of my students out of class. How can I even be sure you're who you say you are?"

Riley rolled her eyes and said, "Look, we could give you our badge numbers and you could check them out with the FBI, but we just don't have time for that."

Crivaro added, "We're investigating the recent murders in this area, including the murder of a student at your school. We've got good reason to believe the killer has abducted another victim. We think Goldie Dowling might be able to help us prevent another murder. But we've got to talk to her *right now*."

A short silence fell.

Then the principal said, "I'll go get her out of class."

"Good," Crivaro said. "We'll need to talk to her privately."

As Riley and her companions waited, Penny let out a quiet moan of despair. She said, "This is my fault. I shouldn't have encouraged her to—"

Riley interrupted, "It's not your fault. You had no idea she might be in any danger."

"I know, but I can't help blaming myself," Penny said.

I know just how you feel, Riley thought.

Penny added, "Oh, please, tell me Larissa is going to be okay."

"We'll do everything we can," Crivaro said. "It helps that we found out so quickly that she's missing. We have you to thank for that."

Then they heard Goldie's voice as she picked up the phone. "Hello?"

Riley said to her, "Goldie, I've got to ask you kind of an awkward question."

"Okay..." Goldie said uneasily.

"Do you know if Kimberly was ever sexually active?"

"What's that got to do with anything?" Goldie asked.

"Maybe a lot—a whole lot," Riley said. "Someone else's life might be at stake right now. We really need for you to be honest with us."

After a pause, Goldie said, "No, she wasn't. Sexually active, I mean. She'd never had sex at all. Neither have I, in case it matters. But for Kimberly...well, it got to be kind of a big deal."

"How do you mean?" Riley asked.

"Well, she signed this stupid pledge," Goldie said. "You see, this counselor came around our school last semester, gave us this lecture about abstinence, tried to get us to sign a pledge to keep ourselves...'pure' was what he called it. I didn't do it. I thought it was stupid. Not many other kids did either. But Kimberly did. She seemed to think it would make her parents happy."

"What happened after that?" Riley asked.

Goldie continued, "Kimberly kind of regretted it later on. It got to be an issue between her and Jay, her boyfriend. Things started to get kind of hot and heavy between them, and Jay really wanted to have sex. The truth is, I think Kimberly kind of wanted the same thing. I think maybe she was thinking about breaking that stupid pledge before Jay broke up with her."

"Who was the guy?" Riley asked. "The one getting kids to sign the pledge?"

"I can't remember his name... Goldie replied. "It was like some kind of a bird."

"Hold on a minute," Riley said. She picked up the newsletter and flipped through the pages. Where had she seen...?

Then she found what she was looking for.

She asked Goldie, "Was it Herron?"

After a moment of hesitation, Goldie replied, "Yeah, that could be it. I'm not sure."

Riley's heart was pounding now.

Maybe we're really on to something, she thought.

She thanked Goldie and ended the call.

Riley realized that Jake and Penny were looking at her expectantly. "The publisher of this newsletter is named Christopher Herron," she told them. "That's the name right here on the masthead. We need to find out if he has other activities as well."

She got to work with Penny's computer and soon came up with an array of books authored by Christopher Herron. She also found a schedule of lecture dates, many of them at schools and churches.

"Have you ever heard of this man?" Riley asked Penny.

"I'm not sure," the receptionist replied. "But guys like that are fairly common around here. They travel around lecturing, talking kids out of having sex. I've heard of ones that get kids to sign pledges, like the girl just told us. A lot of parents think that's terrific."

Riley saw that Crivaro was thumbing idly through the newsletter.

"So Larissa put her personal ad in this clean-living newsletter," he said. "But it doesn't sound like she was looking for complete abstinence in a relationship."

"I think we need to go talk to Christopher Herron," Riley said.

"He should be able to tell us who replied to the ad," Crivaro agreed.

Riley thought in silence for a moment. Pieces of this puzzle were beginning to come together in her head, although they didn't quite fit yet. What was the connection between teenage girls who signed a pledge and a novitiate nun? Or for that matter, with a thirty-two-year-old paralegal looking for a relationship?

Could it be a man who traveled around lecturing teenagers about abstinence?

The newsletter was shaking in her hands.

"I don't think that just anyone read that ad and replied to it," she said. "I think that Christopher Herron is Larissa's mystery date."

CHAPTER TWENTY EIGHT

Christopher clenched his fists, enjoying the feeling of power in his hands. He had strong hands, well suited to their mission. It was all he could do to keep them from strangling the woman—Larissa, she finally admitted was her real name—right this minute.

But I mustn't, he told himself.

Not out of anger.

Only out of necessity.

Only out of mercy.

Only when I have no other choice.

But his fury was rising, and he wasn't sure how much longer he could control himself. He was glad he couldn't see her face in the total darkness. It was bad enough to hear her whining and moaning as she lay bound with duct tape on the floor of his lair.

She's pathetic, he kept thinking.

She's contemptible.

He hadn't felt the same hostility toward any of the others.

He'd been more patient with them.

He'd given them hours and hours and hours to try to make things right.

They'd failed to do that, of course. But he hadn't failed. He'd done his best by them, right to the end. He had to do the same with Larissa.

But could he restrain himself from killing her out of blind rage?

"Please let me go," she kept muttering through sobs. "Please—just let me go."

Struggling to maintain a gentle, kindly tone, he said, "Larissa, I've been trying to explain. I *can* let you go. But only if I can be sure."

"Sure of what?" Larissa wept.

"You know what," he said.

And of course, he was sure she knew perfectly well what he meant.

If she could convince him that she had no intention of ever engaging in sexual relations, he could let her go.

He *would* let her go.

But so far, there seemed little chance of that.

She was crying more quietly now, apparently exhausted from all her wailing and thrashing around. He felt relieved by the comparative quiet. He could hear himself think again.

He leaned back against a wall for a moment to regain his sense of purpose. His mission wasn't about killing. Not at all. It was about preventing suffering, about actually saving lives.

For years he had traveled about this part of the country lecturing on chastity and abstinence. Schools and churches were always eager to host his efforts. And parents were often delighted by the pledges he persuaded young people to sign.

But late last year, something had happened that had convinced him that he had to do more—much more—than simply talk. He had realized that purity had to extend far beyond that simple pledge.

It was Natalie, he remembered.

He'd spoken at her school in Brattledale, and she'd been among the few kids who had eagerly signed the pledge. But afterward, she'd approached him alone and confided her intention to marry a boy named Richard as soon as he got out of the army. He'd been shocked by his own horror at hearing her say this.

After all, Natalie clearly had no intention of breaking her pledge.

The pledge was merely a promise to save herself for marriage, and that was what Natalie still intended to do.

And yet . . .

She was going to lose her purity after all.

What was marriage except an excuse to engage in those loathsome acts?

What was it except a license for unrestrained lust?

Talking with Natalie, he had realized that the pledge alone wasn't sufficient to his purpose. Ever since that conversation, events had seemed to conspire to prove how he was falling short and why he had to do more—much more.

At the high school in Dalhart, a girl named Kimberly—so very much like Natalie—had told him of her plans to get out of her boring hometown and head New York or LA and become an actress.

What will become of her then? he'd wondered at the time.

Under the decadent influences of city life, how long would it be before she forgot her pledge altogether?

He knew he had to do something about her as well.

And finally there was Sandra Hobson—*Sister* Sandra.

He'd spoken at her high school in Trueblood a few years ago, but he'd never forgotten her sparkling innocence and earnestness about holding onto her purity, how happy she'd been to sign his pledge.

He'd been delighted recently to run across her in the streets of nearby Boneau, sweetly dressed in a white habit with a wimple.

She'd chosen to be a nun!

Finally it seemed that he'd found one young woman who had lived up to his hopes and expectations. Sandra had given herself to God, body and soul, and her precious purity would remain forever untouched, just as she had promised in her youth.

Careful to remain unseen, he'd followed her through Boneau, watching her movements. He sensed that she seemed agitated, troubled, restless. Soon he discovered the cause of that restlessness. Sandra went into a local diner, where she met a handsome man about her age. He'd spied them sitting furtively together in an isolated booth, holding hands and whispering to one another passionately.

The shock had almost forced him to accost her right there and then, to stop her from what she was about to do.

She was surely going to forsake her sacred vows, if she hadn't done so already.

Christopher hadn't revealed himself to Sandra then, but he'd felt crushed with a terrible sense of failure. He'd retreated to his well-ordered office and studied his own lecture notes and publications. All three of these young women had heard his words at one time or another. All three had sweetly agreed with him, but now all three of them seemed determined to ruin their lives.

It was then that he'd decided on his course of action—to do his best to redeem them one at a time—Natalie, Kimberly, and Sandra.

But Larissa's case had been different. It was only after he'd made this decision about the others that he'd run across her personal ad in the newsletter that he himself published. She wrote of being "unattached forever," and her meaning had been clear. The fact that she'd placed the ad in *Wholesome Ways* suggested that she was still a virgin.

And thirty-two years old,

It was a beautiful achievement, to have guarded her purity for so many years. And as mature as she was, she surely had some sense of how precious her purity was.

And yet . . .

The wording of the ad made clear that she didn't intend to stay a virgin for long.

Hoping to change all that.

He knew right then that he needed to add her to the list of girls and women he hoped to save from their own carnal desires.

During the last couple of weeks, he'd done his best by Natalie, Kimberly, and Sandra. He'd abducted them with the kindest intentions. One by one they'd failed to convince him that they were going to maintain their purity, so—he'd taken care of that for them.

They would never break their vows now that they were dead.

Now they were fully at peace, immune to all temptations of the flesh.

But now he was wondering whether he'd made a mistake in choosing Larissa.

She was, after all, the only one he'd never met before, the only one who had never signed his pledge at one time or another. Perhaps he shouldn't be surprised that she alone seemed not to have any conception of what he was trying to do for her.

He stooped down and shined a flashlight into her pale, terrified face.

He said, "Don't you understand, I'm trying to save you from a world of pain?"

She blinked and then stared at him dumbly.

Why can't she understand?

He meant it with all his heart. He only wished he could find words to express how deeply and fervently he meant it.

He'd endured so much pain when he was young, inflicted by his own mother whenever he'd been bad—and especially terrible that time when she'd caught him touching himself wickedly. There had been so many burns, cuts, whippings.

He didn't blame his mother, not for a moment.

After all, she'd been trying to redeem him with all these dire punishments.

"You're the cause," she'd told him.

"You're the cause of all my pain."

When he'd gotten old enough, he'd realized how right she was.

He was a man, and inherently loathsome.

He was no different from the man who had inflicted upon his mother the painful and disgusting ordeal of childbirth.

It nauseated him to even think of it.

But so far he'd saved three young souls from his mother's pain.

Surely that lifted some of the vileness from his masculine soul.

And surely there must be something he could still do to help the woman at his feet.

Still exploring her face with the flashlight, he said, "It's your *purity* I want to save. I only want to help you stay pure. Surely you can understand. Surely you can pledge yourself here and now to live a life of purity."

Her mouth moved breathlessly for a moment.

Then she gasped out, "Oh, yes. I understand. I promise. I pledge. I understand completely."

But as he gazed into her eyes, he saw the awful truth about her.

"It's too late," he murmured with regret. "Your very thoughts are sullied."

CHAPTER TWENTY NINE

R iley pushed the little car over the speed limit along the state highway. She wanted to drive even faster, but the last thing she needed right now was to get stopped by some state police officer, particularly while she was driving a civilian vehicle. She couldn't risk losing any time explaining herself to a cop. She believed that a woman's life was probably at stake and that a delay might prove fatal.

It did feel strange, even dangerous, to be heading out on her own like this. But things were happening awfully quickly. Back at the law office, she and Crivaro had been forced to make some hasty decisions.

Jake had called Sheriff Quayle, who had promptly run down two addresses for them—one for the Wholesome Ways business out on a state highway, the other for an apartment where Christopher Herron lived in the nearby town of Rimrock. There was no phone number for the apartment, and there was no answer, not even an answering machine, at the business office.

Riley had insisted they had to get to both places, and fast. That meant she and Crivaro had no choice but to cover each location separately. Quayle had promised to call both the local police and the highway patrol to get them some backup.

With an order to Riley that she was to wait at the office for her backup to arrive, Crivaro had set out to Rimrock in the vehicle they'd been using. Riley had borrowed Penny's car and headed for the Wholesome Ways business location.

As she sped along the state highway, doubts and worries crowded into her mind.

Am I up to this?

It was the question that had plagued her ever since she'd killed Heidi Wright. It was the question Crivaro had kept asking her ever since they'd flown out here from Quantico. And now, if she found the killer and the victim before backup arrived, could she handle the situation alone?

The truth was, she simply didn't know the answer to that question.

She only felt sure of one thing.

I'm not going to kill anyone.

Whatever else she might have to do, she wasn't going to use deadly force.

Not this time.

There has to be another way.

As Riley sped along, she began to wonder if maybe she'd missed the building she was trying to find. The Wholesome Ways business address was on an access road outside of any town. All she'd identified so far were an occasional gas station and a couple of fast food places. Could she have driven right past the publisher's office without realizing it?

But as she rounded a curve, a small building came in sight along the access road to her right. Although no sign was visible from the highway and no cars were parked there, it was the most likely place she'd found so far.

She pulled off the highway onto the access road and drove into the tiny parking lot in front of the building. It was a small, storefront type of structure. And sure enough, it bore a small sign that announced WHOLESOME WAYS. But there was no indication that anyone was there. In fact, when she got out of the car and walked toward the building, she saw a CLOSED sign hanging in the front door.

The whole area felt eerily abandoned.

She stepped close to the big storefront window to get a better look. Several publications were displayed on a shelf just inside the window. One of them was a booklet entitled *Purity*, written by Christopher Herron himself.

Pressing her face against the glass, Riley could see that the office consisted of a single large room. An inside door stood open, revealing a small, empty bathroom. There were some furnishings—a desk, several chairs, bookshelves, filing cabinets, a copy machine. On a long table, neat stacks of brochures, business cards, and small books were lined up in precise rows.

It didn't look like a place where customers were ever expected to come. Instead, it seemed spare, clean, orderly, and efficient. She began to realize that this was really little more than a makeshift base of operations, a place where Herron could manage his publications and organize his lectures and workshops.

From here, he could make Wholesome Ways seem like a much larger enterprise than it really was.

One other thing seemed certain.

There's nobody here.

Riley's heart sank.

She'd driven all the way out here to no purpose, and the cops who were due to arrive soon would have nothing to do.

She could only hope that Crivaro was having better luck.

During the drive to Rimrock, Jake's doubts had started kicking in. Things had seemed much clearer when he, Riley, and Penny had been gathering information back at the law office. They'd managed to positively confirm a connection between Christopher Herron and the second victim, Kimberly Dent.

But what did that really mean?

Now Jake wasn't so sure.

They didn't know for a fact that Natalie Booker had ever signed Herron's pledge, or even whether the girl had actually met him. The same was true for the nun. And the fact Larissa Billham had put a personal ad in Herron's newsletter might not mean anything at all. They had no solid reason to believe it was Herron who had answered the ad, and that he was the man she'd met for a date.

Maybe she'd met some other guy altogether.

For all they really knew, Larissa Billham wasn't really missing at all.

Maybe she's somewhere having a good time right now.

Maybe she just doesn't feel like coming back to work.

There had certainly *seemed* to be some startling connections, but Jake reminded himself of something he still had to remind Riley of from time to time.

Coincidences are a fact of life in this business.

He also didn't feel good about sending Riley off to another location by herself, depending only on the expectation of backup from local police or state troopers. She still seemed awfully fragile, after all.

Maybe she shouldn't even be on this case, he thought yet again.

Maybe I should have sent her home already.

As Jake pulled into Rimrock and drove up to the suspect's address, he drew a breath of relief. He saw a police car parked outside the apartment building, and a couple of cops standing on the steps. The solid, dependable, Quayle had been true to his word and had rousted out backup for them. So Riley would surely be covered too.

Since Jake had driven here from Boneau, he wasn't surprised that the local cops were here ahead of him. But right now they looked awfully conspicuous.

He didn't know how long they'd been standing there, but he was worried that their presence might spook the suspect.

If he really is a suspect.

And if he's there at all.

When he got out of the car, Jake saw that a beefy, bespectacled man was standing there with the two cops. The civilian was smoking a cigar and they all seemed to be having an animated conversation.

Jake hurried up to them and produced his badge and introduced himself.

The cigar-smoking man said, "I'm Horace Benrud, and I own this building. And I'd sure like to know what the hell this is all about."

Jake said, "Do you have a tenant here named Christopher Herron?"

Benrud let out a grunt of disgust.

"I sure do," he said. "What do you want him for?"

"I'd rather not say right now," Jake said. "But I'd like to talk to him."

"Would you, now?" Benrud said. "I'm hoping you want to do a lot more than talk to him. I'd love it if you'd arrest his ass and get him out of my hair once and for all."

Jake was surprised by the animosity in Benrud's voice.

"Has he been giving you trouble?" Jake asked as he and the cops followed Benrud into the building.

"Has he ever," Benrud said. "I'm used to having tenants who party too loud or won't turn down their stereos and TVs. It's moaning and screaming I've got a real problem with. And so do all the people who live on his floor."

Jake's attention was suddenly piqued.

"Moaning and screaming?" he said. "You mean like—?"

"Like somebody in there is in a lot of pain," Benrud said.

Good God, Jake thought.

Maybe he's killing his victims right here in this building.

As they walked up the stairs and continued on down the second story hallway, Jake could see what a rundown building this was. He guessed that it had once been a fairly nice small-town hotel, but that had surely been a long time ago. Since then it all the rooms had been turned into low-rent apartments.

Jake thought about what little he knew about Christopher Herron—that he published a newsletter, and that he toured around churches and high schools giving lectures about chastity. Jake had assumed that he must be a reasonably successful businessman. This was hardly the sort of place where Jake would have expected him to live.

They arrived at the apartment, and Jake knocked sharply on the door.

He called out, "Christopher Herron, this is Special Agent Jake Crivaro of the FBI. I'd like to have a word with you."

There was no reply.

Jake felt a tingle of apprehension.

He asked the landlord, "When was the last time anybody heard any noises from in there?"

"I'm not sure," Benrud said with a shrug. "I haven't had any complaints so far today. That doesn't mean it hasn't been going on. It's more like the tenants are getting tired of complaining."

As Jake stared at the door, his imagination filled with terrible possibilities.

He might be in there with Larissa, he thought.

If so, the victim was being awfully quiet.

Perhaps she was already dead.

Jake said to Benrud, "I need to get in this room. I've got reason to think that violent crimes have been committed in there. There might be a murder in progress."

Benrud's eyes widened.

"Jesus," he said. "I wouldn't be surprised, but..."

Benrud paused and squinted uneasily at the door.

Jake braced himself for having to talk the landlord into letting him into the room without a warrant. If Jake's suspicions were the least bit true, they didn't have time to deal with a judge.

Then Benrud grunted and said, "Okay, let's do this thing."

Benrud produced a key and opened the door. Benrud and Jake stepped inside, followed by the two cops.

The apartment was even smaller than Jake had expected, with a tiny built-in kitchen and an unmade bed that doubled as a sofa. The place was filthy and cluttered. The sink was piled high with dirty dishes, and other plates with uneaten food were lying all about. There were also pamphlets and booklets scattered all over the place. At a glance, Jake could see that some of them were authored by Herron himself.

Then Jake heard one of the cops speak up.

"Hey, Agent Crivaro. You'd better have a look at this."

Jake turned and saw that the cop was standing beside an open closet, looking a bit queasy.

Even Jake was startled by what he saw inside.

The closet was full of what appeared to be instruments of pain—a multi-corded whip, a hair shirt, a spiked collar and garters, a car battery with cables, and what looked like an electric cattle prod.

Benrud growled, "Well, I guess now we know what all the screaming's been about."

Jake silently agreed. There was no sign of a victim anywhere—indeed, no sign that anybody ever came to this room except the man who lived here. Jake felt sure that Christopher Herron used these devices purely for his own pain and mortification.

He's a sick, sick man, Jake thought.

Jake also had no doubt that Herron was the killer they were looking for.

Riley stood there staring through the window for a few more moments, hoping to catch a glimpse of something that would tell her more about the owner. Surely there would be something here to reveal the dark side of the man who published these materials. But she saw nothing to suggest that anything violent had ever taken place here. It seemed to be nothing more than a very orderly place of business.

There's no point in staying here, she thought.

She figured she might as well notify Quayle to call off the backup. Then she'd check in with Crivaro and find out whether he was having better luck in Rimrock.

But as the turned away from the Wholesome Ways office, Riley decided to have a look around the entire outside of the little building. She walked around a corner and toward the back. When she reached the area behind the office, something came into view that made her stop in shock.

A white utility van was parked there.

It was very much like the groundskeeper's vehicle she'd seen last night at Magdalene High School—the kind of van she'd theorized that the killer might use to abduct his victims.

She could see no one in the driver's or passenger's seat. But the back had no windows.

She dashed over to the van and pounded on the side door.

"This is the FBI," she yelled. "Open up this vehicle."

She didn't hear the slightest sound in reply. She tugged on the side door handle and was surprised that the door slid readily open.

No one was in the back part of the van either.

But the interior was exactly what she'd expected. The bed of the van was entirely bare, and it was separated from the front two seats by a sturdy wire mesh. There wasn't a doubt in her mind that this was the very vehicle the killer had used to abduct his victims—and that Christopher Herron was that killer.

But where was he now?

And where was Larissa Billham?

Riley whirled back toward the Wholesome Ways building. She saw that a tiny stairwell led down to a basement door.

Her heart was pounding now.

He's in there.

So is she.

I'm sure of it.

But had she arrived too late to save the woman's life?

A faint voice in her mind echoed Crivaro's order to wait for her backup to arrive. But what if she waited and another woman died?

Riley crept down the stairs until she stood just outside the door. She knew better than to knock or call out. She didn't want to give any warning of her arrival. Instead, she turned the doorknob, and the door creaked open.

She found herself staring into total darkness. She drew her weapon, took her penlight out of her handbag, and stepped through the doorway into the basement.

Before Riley could see anything in the beam of light, she was knocked to the floor by a strong shove from behind her. The door slammed shut, the light went out, and she couldn't see a thing.

She heard a sinister voice speak to her in the darkness.

"You shouldn't be here."

CHAPTER THIRTY

Still gripping her gun, Riley tried to scramble to her feet in the darkness. Her penlight was gone, and she'd lost any sense of her position in the room. A constant soft weeping and moaning from somewhere in the dark obscured the fainter sounds of someone moving about.

Then came another blow—a much harder and sharper blow from a hard object to the back of her head. The darkness seemed to explode with bright lights and she heard her gun clatter to the concrete floor.

Riley was afraid she might lose consciousness.

Hold it together, she told herself.

She managed to stagger to her feet, but she had no idea where the door leading outside might be. She felt as if she were in some endless ocean of blackness.

Then she heard the man's voice again. He was somewhere in front of her now.

"You're not supposed to be here. Who are you? What are you doing here?"

"Are you Christopher Herron?" she asked, surprised at the foggy sound of her own voice.

There was a brief silence. Then he asked again more sharply, "What are you doing here?"

Riley struggled to hold onto consciousness, but she was gripped by waves of confusion.

She found herself wondering . . .

Here? What am *I doing here?*

Was this another nightmare?

Then she heard another voice, a woman's, cry out in the darkness.

"Help me. Whoever you are, please help me."

Everything seemed less real by the moment.

Who's calling for help? Riley wondered in her confusion.

Is that Heidi Wright?

Or Sister Sandra?

Or is it . . . ?

Whoever she was, the woman was weeping bitterly and fearfully.

Then came a burst of blinding white light, and Riley reflexively shielded her eyes. In a couple of seconds, she realized that her assailant had switched on a flashlight shining directly into her face. She thought it must be what he'd struck her with a moment ago.

I know where he is now, she thought hopefully.

But when she reached for her weapon, it wasn't in her holster.

What had happened to it?

Hadn't she been holding it when she came in here?

She vaguely remembered hearing it clatter to the floor when she was struck across the head.

Then a peculiar realization passed through her mind.

It doesn't matter.

I couldn't use it anyway.

But why couldn't she use it?

Had she become incapable of using deadly force?

Riley's own thoughts made no sense to her.

Knowing she had to take some action, she lunged in the direction of the light. But the man easily dodged out of the way

A new wave of dizziness swept over Riley and she almost tumbled back to the floor. While she struggled to stay on her feet, he pinned her face again under the flashlight beam.

Then the man spoke to Riley in a surprisingly gentle voice.

"Oh, you poor soul. You've come to me for help, haven't you? You want me to save you from corruption. But I can see in your face, it's too late for you. You've lost everything. You've lost your purity. Everything that was ever good about you is gone."

A tide of irrational thoughts rose up inside Riley.

Try as she might to hang onto some slender thread of reason, she couldn't help thinking he was right.

I've failed at everything.

I've let everybody down.

"There's only one thing left I can do for you," the man said.

Then he tossed the flashlight aside and lunged ferociously at Riley. She was too weak and disoriented to put up any kind of a fight, and he quickly had his hands around her throat. She couldn't breathe, and she felt a deep tingling through her skull as the blood flow to her head ebbed away.

As she writhed and twisted in throes of final desperation, Riley glimpsed the captive lying on the floor, bound hand and foot with duct tape. The beam of the fallen flashlight was shining on the victim she'd come here hoping to save. The woman stared at Riley with a pleading expression, as if to say again:

"Please help me."

Riley was overcome with guilt as her last ounce of consciousness began to slip away.

She'd failed Heidi, and then Sister Sandra, and now this woman.

I can't help her, she thought.

I can't help anybody.

I've failed.

Familiar images took over her mind.

The darkness that surrounded Riley turned into a heavy swirl of falling snow.

Riley realized she was back at the scene of the shootout in New York State.

But for a moment, she couldn't see anything through the dense snowfall.

Then she could see a shadowy figure approaching her.

As the figure came closer, Riley gasped to realize who it was.

"Heidi Wright!" she exclaimed.

For a moment, her heart leapt with hope.

Was it possible that she hadn't killed Heidi after all?

Had that only been some bad dream?

But then she saw the gaping, bleeding wound in Heidi's chest, and the girl's eyes stared blankly at her. Riley's heart sank bitterly. Heidi was dead after all. And Riley had killed her.

Her assailant's words from a few moments ago seemed to echo in the air.

"Everything that was ever good about you is gone."

It's true, Riley thought.

And she could think of no way to get any of her lost goodness back.

But then she saw that Heidi's lips were moving.

What's she saying? *Riley wondered.*

The wind was whistling now, and Heidi's voice was too weak to hear, but soon Riley found that she could read the girl's lips as she repeated again and again . . .

"Thank you. Thank you. Thank you."

Riley was dumbfounded. What on earth could Heidi be thanking her for?

She could now hear Heidi whisper as if in reply.

"For caring."

Those words hit Riley like a thunderbolt of realization.

Now she understood completely.

Riley had cared about Heidi's fate. She'd even grieved for the poor girl. She'd empathized with Heidi in death more than almost anyone had during the girl's whole sad life. Riley had cared, too, for Sister Sandra, and felt deeply for her loss.

Suddenly the world seemed wonderfully warm, despite the falling snow.

Riley almost laughed at how she'd worried about losing her humanity.

As long as she could feel such deep sorrow for another living soul, she'd always be fully alive . . .

And human.

Heidi smiled as if she could read Riley's thoughts.

Before she turned and walked back into the snowfall, she said one more word to Riley.

"Fight."

Despite the man's hands clenched around her throat, Riley felt a renewed surge of consciousness.

She remembered vividly the last word Heidi had spoken to her.

"Fight."

And that was exactly what Riley had to do right now.

She summoned her strength and lifted her knee, landing a sharp blow to the man's groin. With a groan of agony, he tumbled off her, bumping into the flashlight and whirling it around on the floor so that its beam shone wildly and fleetingly in all directions.

As the man struggled to regain his footing, he was staring at something that glittered in the scattering light. It was Riley's fallen weapon.

He snatched it from the floor and stood up, pointing the gun directly at her.

"I'll help you yet," he snarled. "Only in death can you regain your precious purity."

Riley felt a brief spasm of fear.

I'm going to die now.

But then she smiled. In her confusion a few moments ago she'd dimly and strangely believed she couldn't use the gun.

Now she remembered exactly why.

Her assailant pulled the trigger, and nothing happened.

He clicked the trigger again and again.

Then he stared at the gun as if it had personally betrayed him.

Riley actually laughed. Before coming here, determined to finish this case without killing anyone, she had removed the cartridge from her gun.

Drawing her weapon upon entering this basement had only been a bluff. And Christopher Herron had now fallen for that bluff more fully than she could have hoped.

Energy flowed back into Riley's limbs and she scrambled to her feet. She charged the killer, drew back her fist, and slammed it into his face. Dazed, he tottered onto his knees. Riley deftly began to put him into handcuffs as he knelt helplessly on the basement floor.

Just then, Riley heard the sound of vehicles pulling up to the building.

The police had arrived.

She looked at the woman who still lay bound on the floor.

"Don't worry," Riley said. "We're getting you out of here."

Then she added, as much to herself as to the woman, "You're going to be all right."

CHAPTER THIRTY ONE

Jake felt a calmness settling over him as he watched through the jet window at the Tennessee farmland rolling slowly by far below.

So peaceful, he thought.

He breathed long and slowly. The tranquil landscape and the friendly rumble of the jet engine were a welcome relief after all that had happened recently. In the distance he could see a glint of sunlight off the smooth, untroubled surface of the Mississippi River.

But of course, Jake knew that those waters hid powerful and sometimes dangerous undercurrents.

Just like the rest of the world, Jake thought.

And in a way, just like Christopher Herron, whose friendly and righteous demeanor had inspired people's trust and admiration for many years until...

Jake shuddered as he remembered Herron's crazed ranting after his arrest and during his initial questioning. Much of it had made little sense to Jake or anyone else. But at least it was clear that Herron's childhood mistreatment by his twisted, puritanical mother had left wounds that had festered for many years until they had finally erupted into murderous acts.

Jake felt confident that the whole truth would emerge in a short time.

And at least it's an open-and-shut case, Jake thought.

Herron had been caught red-handed with his last intended victim, after all. And Jake was sure that plenty of proof was still to follow, including physical evidence from Herron's van and the basement of his office.

Jake's musings were interrupted when Riley spoke from the seat next to his.

"Agent Crivaro, something's bugging me."

Jake chuckled a little.

"I hope it's nothing too dire," he said. "I've had enough excitement for one day."

Riley paused for a moment before she said, "I was wrong."

"About what?" Jake asked.

"Yesterday my instincts told me that the killer hated religion, and that's what was driving him. But that didn't turn out to be the truth at all. It was something completely different."

Jake shrugged and said, "That doesn't mean your instincts were bad. Sometimes even a mistaken hunch can be useful. At least that hunch got us moving in the right direction. And you did get it right in the end, when you figured out that the victims were all virgins."

"Yeah, I guess," Riley said. "But still..."

Her voice faded away.

The Jake said, "Actually, on the whole, you were pretty damned brilliant."

Riley's face broke into a broad smile.

"Do you really think so?" she said.

"I know so," Jake said.

Then he wagged his finger at her and added, "You've still got to see a shrink, though."

"Don't worry, I'll do that."

"And what were you thinking, going in there with an unloaded gun?"

"It won't happen again."

"It damn well better not happen again."

The two of them fell into a comfortable silence. The truth was, Jake was no longer worried about Riley's emotional strength and resiliency. Somehow or other—he really didn't know just how—she had fully recovered from the trauma of shooting Heidi Wright. Seeing a shrink would be little more than a formality.

She's going to be just fine, he thought.

He wasn't so sure about himself, though.

He knew perfectly well that he couldn't have solved this case on his own, or with a less talented partner. He needed Riley's help to be anywhere near as good as he used to be.

And what about the near future? If his own powers were declining, would he soon be a drag on Riley's abilities to do her job? Was he maybe getting to be a drag on her already? Didn't she deserve to team up with a partner more nearly matched to her intelligence and ability?

Jake couldn't help but laugh to himself.

Finding her match won't be easy, he thought.

For now, I'll just have to do.

He closed his eyes, wondering just what retirement might mean for him. After so many years as a field agent, he really couldn't imagine it. For the time being, he looked forward with apprehension to the murder trial of Larry Mullins. He still felt as though he'd fallen short on that case.

Well, there will be a verdict, one way or the other.

He decided that the verdict wouldn't be solely about Mullins's guilt or innocence.

It would be about his own abilities as well.

It would determine whether it was time for him to pack it in and quit.

Riley couldn't stop smiling as the Virginia scenery whipped past the train window. She was on her way home, and she couldn't remember the last time she'd felt this happy.

For one thing, her psych evaluation back in Quantico had cleared her for service once and for all. The therapist did scold Riley for going back on the job without getting the mandatory examination. He also had some harsh words for Crivaro and Erik Lehl for letting her get away with it. But given everything Riley had been through, the therapist was actually surprised that she was doing so well.

I'm glad he didn't see me yesterday, she thought.

She hadn't tried to explain to the therapist that she'd had some kind of personal revelation while a madman was trying to strangle her to death. She figured that would sound too weird.

Anyway, Riley felt sufficiently content to get an official clean bill of mental health.

Sane at last, she thought.

Of course, she knew that sanity was a relative term. Her own brand of sanity seemed to be at least partly founded on dreams and hallucinations, sometimes about dead people. She figured it was probably best not to get into all that with a therapist.

Or maybe anybody else, for that matter.

She'd called ahead to let Ryan to let him know she'd finished the case and was on her way home, and he'd sounded happy and relieved. Of course she knew they still had a lot of things to talk about and unresolved issues and tensions. Still, she hoped that maybe the clouds that had been darkening their relationship lately were starting to lift at last.

When the train pulled into the DC station, Riley was surprised to see Ryan waiting for her on the platform, looking like the handsome and charming young man she had fallen in love with in the first place. She'd assumed that she'd have to make her way to their apartment on her own. This was a delightful surprise.

When he took her into his arms, Riley felt as though she might melt from sheer joy.

Then he asked, "Did you catch the bad guy?"

Riley was startled.

What a quaint way to put it, she thought.

Ryan clearly didn't have a clue of what she'd been through during the last couple of days.

But maybe it's just as well.

Maybe some things were best left unsaid.

"Yeah, I did," she said. "Or Crivaro and I did, anyway."

"Good for you," Ryan said. "I'm proud of you."

Then he stepped back and looked her over.

"Oh, my," he said. "You're not at all dressed for tonight."

"What's going on tonight?" Riley asked.

"I've got a reservation for the two of us at Hugo's Embers. I hope that's okay."

Riley laughed.

We're going to have that romantic evening after all.

She just hoped she wasn't too tired to enjoy it.

"Of course it's okay," she said. "Now take me home so I can get cleaned up and properly attired."

As they headed out of the station toward the car, Ryan said, "We do have something serious to discuss over dinner, though."

"What is it?" Riley asked.

"Let's talk about it over some glasses of good wine."

Riley was swept by a deep and comfortable sense of warmth. She knew Ryan well, and she knew what he had in mind. He wanted to set a wedding date at last.

And so do I.

It felt as though life was off to a fresh new start.

Riley only hoped this happiness could last.

Now Available for Pre-Order!

KILLING
(The Making of Riley Paige–Book 6)

"A masterpiece of thriller and mystery! The author did a magnificent job developing characters with a psychological side that is so well described that we feel inside their minds, follow their fears and cheer for their success. The plot is very intelligent and will keep you entertained throughout the book. Full of twists, this book will keep you awake until the turn of the last page."

—Books and Movie Reviews, Roberto Mattos (re Once Gone)

KILLING (The Making of Riley Paige—Book Six) is book #6 in a new psychological thriller series by #1 bestselling author Blake Pierce, whose free bestseller Once Gone (Book #1) has over 1,000 five star reviews.

When victims are found killed by electrocution, it is up to the FBI's brilliant new agent, Riley Paige, 22, to enter a serial killer's warped mind and stop him before he can claim any more victims.

Riley, fresh out of the academy and off her last case, is settling into FBI life when a shocking twist threatens her partnership with her mentor, Jake, and undermines everything she thought she knew.

Can Riley keep her personal life under control while trying to catch a diabolical killer at the same time?

An action-packed thriller with heart-pounding suspense, KILLING is book #6 in a riveting new series that will leave you turning pages late into the night. It takes readers back 20 plus years—to how Riley's career began—and is the perfect complement to the ONCE GONE series (A Riley Paige Mystery), which comprises 17 books.

KILLING
(The Making of Riley Paige—Book 6)

Did you know that I've written multiple novels in the mystery genre? If you haven't read all my series, click the image below to download a series starter!

Made in United States
Orlando, FL
12 October 2023

37810902R00125